TOO OLD TO DANCE BUT YOUNG ENOUGH TO ROCK 'N' ROLL

....

I0660128

L. GENE BROWN
AND
K. CERES WRIGHT

MVmedia, LLC
Fayetteville, Georgia

MVmedia, LLC
PO Box 143052
Fayetteville, GA
www.mvmediaatl.com

Publisher's Note: This is a work of fiction. Names, characters, places, and incidents are a product of the author's imagination. Locales and public names are sometimes used for atmospheric purposes. Any resemblance to actual people, living or dead, or to businesses, companies, events, institutions, or locales is completely coincidental.

Book Layout ©2017 BookDesignTemplates.com

Ordering Information:
Quantity sales. Special discounts are available on quantity purchases by corporations, associations, and others. For details, contact the "Special Sales Department" at the address above.

Too Old to Dance but Young Enough to Rock 'n' Roll/ L. Gene Brown and K. Ceres Wright. -- 1st ed.
ISBN 979-8-9905120-1-6

Contents

Dear Reader: Science fiction can serve as a warning to veer from an impending course of action, or as a guide toward the beacon of a desired goal. I believe peace is always a beacon that can be achieved through foresight and diplomacy. Please weigh your leaders' commitment to peace and vote accordingly.
-K Ceres Wright

Chapter 1
Valiant

Call me Val. It's short for Valiant, meaning possessing or acting with bravery, boldness, and courage. It's more a title, an identifier, actually, given to me in the days following my field commission to Lieutenant in the USEF—the United States Expeditionary Forces. The full, official designation, to date, is Captain Valiant, C-in-C, Fourth Battalion, Foxtrot Company, Second Platoon of the USEF.

To be dead-on accurate, the name I was given at birth was ValJean. One I haven't heard in a very long time.

I was just a boy back in 2037, six months shy of my tenth birthday when the wars began. Back when there were still televisions, cell phones, and a worldwide Internet, and as far as that goes, whole, undecimated cities. Back before sanity called a time-out and the Super Powers, and the wannabe powers, and everybody capable, decided to rain nuclear fire down on. . .everybody.

That was 25 years ago—give or take six months or so. Since that time, I have seen and experienced things that have run the gamut, horrific to tragic (the deaths of my parents, siblings, and friends), chilling to incredulous, savage to nightmarish.

Most recently, the year-long Battle of the Lowlands in Glasgow, Scotland, and the 2½-year Berlin Siege against very well-trained and well-equipped elements of the Russo–China Coalition—the Red Storm.

AlliedCom—the surviving and combined military brain trusts of the USA, UK, Israel, and the French and German Federations. What remains of the news media called them, 'hard fought and gallant stands against insurmountable odds. . .decisive victories.' The realistic version: They ran out of food and ammunition before we did.

The ravages of war may have had its deleterious effects on several aspects of world culture, but one thing, *bullshit*, remained unchanged.

#

Commander's Journal
July 25, 2062
2145 hours

Day 121. Roughly four months since the Second and Third Platoons were secretly inserted into Sector 001, the Canadian Provinces once known as Montréal.

We began with a complement of 84 men and women and a full contingent of equipment and materiel. In the time it has taken us to make our way through the Canadian wilderness to America's Eastern Seaboard—through skirmishes with wild animal packs and a number of rebel and guerilla elements—our numbers have been substantially diminished. So, too, have our stores of ammunition and rations. We are now operating in the realm of what my XO likes to call the 'Banana Peel and the Grave Scenario.' And I wish to God I could disagree.

Too Old To Dance . . .

Today marks the third day, hour 74 to be exact, since our arrival in the Washington, DC, Hot Zone—Sector Golf, Georgetown, and the inner-rim of the District proper. We set up a temporary base camp in what's left of a two-story stone house (what had once been a bed & breakfast) and its large rear courtyard along the water-front—having reached our planned destination less than a week ahead of schedule—and will adjust our position (whenever the need arises), running recon and regular area patrols until the next SatCom check-in with Allied HQ or contact with our Allied Intelligence advance element, code name FireDrake.

"Permission to enter." The instantly recognizable voice of my second-in-command prompted me to close, roll up, and stow my battered leather-bound notebook.

"Come," I replied. I looked up from the severely pitted dining room table that served as my desk to greet the entrance of the aforementioned—Captain Athena, aka Sunny.

"Gimme a minute?" She plucked the sweat-stained bandana off her short-cropped blonde head and veered away from the table, gesturing to a second table at my left-rear, where an old-fashioned Igloo water cooler and a number of plastic cups waited.

I nodded in response, watching as she filled a cup to its brim and gulped noisily.

Funny, the things your mind chooses to seize on at certain moments. Athena and I had been comrades-in-arms for well over a decade. Had cut our combat-teeth in the campaigns of San Diego, San Francisco, and Seattle. And through it all, she'd never been more than just that. . .a fellow soldier. Eventually, a chosen member of my command staff, and as time and events progressed, a trusted friend.

Looking at her now, it suddenly dawned on me that there was a person underneath the mileage, the dirt- and sweat-etched wrinkles, and the dark combat BDUs. Like me, there was another life. . .a family, past hopes, and dreams. Someone I didn't really know at all.

"Woosh!" She finally turned away from the cooler, fanning herself. "Sunset was two hours ago and it's still hot enough to boil water out there."

I almost laughed. "The middle of July, sixty-seven percent ozone depletion, and you expected what. . .a spring day in Iowa?"

"I'd settle for hailstorms and tornadoes in Kansas. But this. . .? Jesus waffles." She used the bandana to dab at her sweat-beaded brow, trudging across the room's dirt-caked and shrapnel-pockmarked carpet to pull up one of the packing crates we'd been using for chairs.

"Sitrep?" I queried once she'd settled in.

"You've got a choice this time." She held up three fingers, "Good news, bad news, and bad-to-shitty news. Any order you prefer?"

"What won't upset my delicate sensibilities?"

"All right, then. Good first, or at least as good as it gets. All three recon patrols are back. No hard contact with hostile forces, so no casualties.

12

"I'm gonna lump the bad and bad-to-shitty into one package. First, Alpha Team observed at least four camps bivouacked around the District. Seventy-five personnel all totaled. Weapons and insignia identify them as *November Dawn*—Israeli SpecOps."

"Rogue Israeli," I corrected, as if the distinction made the slightest shred of difference. "And there's worse. . .shittier news than that?"

Sunny heaved a tight-lipped shrug. "Six more desertions since last night. Young troops, probably grew up in this area and took off looking for surviving family. The problem is, they took weapons, ammo, and a big chunk of rations with them. Food-wise, if we parse what we have to half rations, we might be able to stretch it out for a month. As far as ammo, if we run into the same level of contact with hostiles as we did with the rebels in Canada, and excuse my French, we're fucked."

"Jesus," I groaned softly.

"I'm fairly sure he's not taking any calls lately," Sunny quipped. "Or the Man above him, as far as that goes. I'd say we're on our own."

Sunny being an avowed atheist, her assessment of the situation was understandable. Myself, on the other hand, the product of a long family line of Baptist upbringing, at any other time I might have argued with her. But after everything that had happened, all we'd experienced the past few weeks, holding onto my faith was like stacking marbles in a corner. A very delicate and iffy proposition, to be sure.

BROWN, WRIGHT

Chapter 2
Zana

Carver Langston Neighborhood
Washington, DC
July 25, 2062
1545 hours

Gunshots staccatoed above our heads as the Blue Team and I hunkered down behind wrecks of abandoned and rusted-out cars. We were taking fire in the middle of G Street NE after a manhole mine took out our Jeep's front end and we got out to look at it. We scattered toward cover as shots ricocheted off the Jeep's bulletproof armoring. Better five smaller targets than one large one. I strained to shout orders above the cacophony and my own return fire. Empty townhouses looked down on the scene with broken-glass eyes.

"Call Red and Gold Teams!"

We'd been on our way back from an exchange meeting with the New IRA in the arboretum—our fuel in exchange for their MREs. While surveying Kingman Park with ground-penetrating radar, we had discovered three tanks from abandoned gas stations, all of which still held fuel that could be used with hybrid vehicles. So, we had gas but were running out of food. We had proposed a trade, only we didn't know the gang, the Red Dogs, had taken the Carver Langston area.

Lady Luck had ridden with us to the arboretum but hopped off on the way back. Now we were shooting our way back to base in Kingman Park.

I peered out from behind an overturned Chevy truck and spied several dead gang members laid out in the street.

"Seren!"

My gaze tracked left, where Turai Cohen crouched, holding a DMS assault rifle. He'd been a new transfer from Israel, with this likely being his first real firefight, and I worried he might freeze in the melee. I tried to reassure him.

"Hold on, Cohen. We'll make it."

My worries vanished as Red and Gold Teams arrived, raining down a barrage of high-explosive hell. The nearby buildings exploded as brick and concrete disintegrated in bursts of dust. Brass shell casings from mounted guns bounced off the pavement as they caught the sun's glint, sparkling like found treasure. Time slowed, as if we'd been caught in a small frame of forever, then sped up as the sound of fire faded. Urban warfare at its finest. I silently thanked the IDF doctor who had bathed my eardrums in hearing-preserving nanites.

"C'mon!" Samal Levy motioned to us to get our asses in gear and we crouch-ran to his Jeep as he opened the door and hauled us in. Gold Team provided cover and I'd never been more relieved to see its leader, Segen Omer. *The asshole.*

With everyone inside, I palmed the external com and announced, "Let's go!" We skidded out past the rows of townhouses with their jagged concrete and rebar poking up through the rubble. Light poles that were either bent to the ground or snapped in half lined our exit route, standing sentinel over lawns that looked as if they had undergone a Brazilian wax job. It was the same, block after block, with an occasional house that still stood whole, lone representatives of the Time Before. As we sped down the street, I looked forward to a cold shower and a hot MRE.

Personal Journal
July 25, 2062
1905 hours
"It's not the heat, it's the humidity," I once said on my first visit to Washington, DC. Now it's both. I don't even bother with perms or flat irons anymore, opting instead for twists, with what's left of my hair. I'd heard of a Black American soldier who had been captured by a tribal lord in Syria. He looked through her pack and asked what all the bottles and jars were. "My hair products," she said. I can relate. The women in Africa have an abundance of ochre. I am on my last jar of petroleum jelly I looted from the back of an abandoned drug store. With the high radiation levels, we're all going to go bald and die early anyway. I just want to look halfway decent when it's my time to go.

On another note, our food supplies are diminishing. Water is plentiful, being near the Potomac River, but we are running out of filters. As there is not much manufacturing in the DC area, I might have to send a man to Columbia to raid the closest factory. No one wants to drink the Potomac unfiltered.

I closed my journal, had a cold shower, and ate an MRE I heated on a can of sterno as I contemplated the day's events, especially the fuck up on G Street. I'd have to talk to the boys in tech about improving our mine detectors. It seemed every time we clawed our way to having an advantage, enemies would find a way around it, and the whole cycle would begin again. But the important thing was my troops' morale had been lifted. . .and we lived to fight another day.

#

Segen Bichler's Tent
Kingman Park Neighborhood
1910 hours
"Message for Seren Nizana Nahome Shalom, Unit 212, 89th Oz Brigade, 98th Division, Central Command."

I turned to face Cohen, who was standing with slumped shoulders in the tent's open flap. He was silhouetted against the sun, a black figure holding a pad.

"Stop being a smartass," I said.

I hadn't heard someone say my full name since my mother used it the last time I saw her. She had been admonishing me about my bad habits of drinking and screwing guys I hardly knew. Good Jewish girls didn't do that. And it was important that I be good, because Temple, even though I hadn't been in 3 years. She'd outright disown me if she found out I'd converted to

Christianity. I was dreading that meeting…if we ever made it back to Israel.

When we Ethiopian Jews, or Beta Israel, had emigrated to Israel, we were told to choose new names to reflect our new life. Some families had chosen Jewish last names, some the first name of their grandfather as their new last name. My family had done both, so my great-great-grandfather's name was now my middle name, and Shalom my last.

My second in command, Segen Levi Bichler, met my blank gaze and stood up from his desk.

"I'll take it."

His words broke my reverie.

Cohen handed Levi the pad and jogged away. "What is it?"

Levi handed me the pad. It was a satellite communication message:

NOTICE ADVISORY TO OFEK 25 USERS (NAOU) 3083996

START TIME ZULU: 1300

STOP TIME ZULU: 1900

TIME RECEIVED: 1314

TO: SEREN SHALOM, 89/98/CC

FROM: ALUF MISHNE EPSTEIN CC/GS

MESSAGE: INTEL RECD EGY & PAK. AWAIT US. ALERT P45. NEW ALLIED MISSION SUSPECTED: CON-FIRM.

Levi looked at me expectantly. The Israel Defense Forces had been just that…defensive. Traditionally, we had pledged no territorial ambitions and typically did not deploy. Yes, we had the world's most technologically advanced army because we were always fighting, but we didn't have the troop numbers other armies had. We protected Israel, its borders, and its people. That was it. But the war had changed all that. Now we had been tasked with gathering intel that would help protect Israel from anywhere around the globe. Egypt, and distantly, Pakistan, were thought to hold advanced weaponry, but recon intelligence from our previous mission indicated their defense systems were in disarray.

The message confirmed Central Command had received that information and awaited intel about the USA, especially on Protocol 45, the supposed thing that would end the war. No one really knew what it was, only that it existed, in some form or shape. If the Allies were seen changing tactics, most likely relating to P45, I had just been given the task of finding out why.

My team had played up the rumor that we had gone rogue, ignoring Central Command, our commanding officers, and Israel, in general, and giving ourselves the new name of November Dawn. In reality, we still worked as a cohesive unit for the IDF, gathering intel where and how we could. Even now, four of our units were bivouacked around the District, but four more were running recon in the bushes, sewers, and whatever other hidey-hole they could make or find. I would need to impress our new orders on them.

I met Levi's gaze. "We're under orders to find out what we can about Protocol 45 and the Allied coalition's plans. Send Mizrahi to me. I'll be in my tent drawing up a strategy."

"Yes, ma'am."

I strode outside and took a quick glance at the charred landscape. Burned tree stumps jutted up from the jigsaw of cracked, hardened earth, dotted with random patches of brown grass. I sighed and walked to my tent, forcing my mind to think on strategy and not our increasingly hopeless plight. Good intel had been hard to come by, and it'd been a few months since I had heard of any to be had. Foreign troops, as well as the IDF, seemed to just be circling around Washington, DC, as if waiting on…something. Was it P45? Or was it death by radiation? I put the thought from my mind. I washed my face with water from my canteen and dried it with the bottom half of my shirt. In this heat, it would be dry in no time.

Mizrahi jogged up and slumped against the tent pole, as if he'd just outrun the ROK Army. A series of data nodes lay in rows on his scalp, poking up just above his short-cropped hair.

"You wanted to see me?"

"Yeah, start up the generator and check the other countries' comms about Protocol 45. I need to know where these rumors are coming from. Who keeps putting these hints and clues out there? The Americans? Chinese? Root around and see what you can find."

"Yes, ma'am." Mizrahi lifted himself off the tent pole and jogged away.

Whoever was leaving clues about P45 had all the factions by the short hairs. Most everyone wanted the war to be over, except for some psychopaths who got off on suffering and mayhem. And the war had made plenty of those.

Chapter 3
Of Lions and Pork Chops

INCOMING: Satellite Communiqué
AUTH.CODE: Allied Command – Camelot
ENCRYPTION PROTOCOL: Lexicon 4 –
Excalibur
DOWNLOAD/RECORD: Active

FROM: Mercury, Major, Camelot – AI-7, AL-
LIED   INTELLIGENCE
TO: Valiant, Colonel, Commander Operation
DragonFire
Dispatch As Follows –

Item 1 – Confirmed; Mission
intel compromised. Enemy factions cognizant.
Item 2 – As of 1545 hours
07/26/2062, Third Platoon met
with heavy resistance by over-
whelming forces. No longer able
to rendezvous with your command.
Item 3 – Be advised. Euro The-
ater now under Defense Order
OMEGA. Time to institution: 1
Week 36 Hours 15 Minutes.

Dispatch Ends.

#

Commander's Journal
July 27, 2062
2100 hours

Day 123. Can't say I was surprised by the contents of my last SatCom from AI-7. First of all, Captain Galahad's Third Platoon should have radioed to confirm their rendezvous a full 48 hours ago. And the fact that they didn't meant only one thing—they had either been wiped out, down to the last man or woman, or captured, or both.

Second—"Mission intel compromised" more than affirmed reports from my recon patrols. They identified elements of at least four military factions in and around the greater DC area. The most formidable of which being November Dawn. Most recent intel had them sighted in both Egypt and Pakistan. I would be naïve to believe that their presence here, now, is a coincidence.

And lastly, Defense Order Omega, the countdown to total surrender of Allied Forces in Europe. An inevitable probability. Throughout the war, alliances had shifted, some completely erased, while others were absorbed into larger, more powerful factions. Realistically, it was only a matter of time before one of the major powers conquered the other. Hence the reason for Operation DragonFire. Which makes its success even more imperative.

#

A soft breeze wafted in through the jury-rigged veil (a swatch of bayonet-shredded shower curtain) over the window—or what had once been a window—beside my makeshift bed. It carried with it the slight scents of jasmine and honeysuckle, overshadowed, however, by the lingering stench of ruin and decay. An unrelenting reminder of life and the current times.

"Damn shame there's no 'lectricity." The statement interrupted my brief introspective funk, calling my attention to the sparsely dressed figure moving toward me from the sideboard across the room. Bathed in the pale flicker of a single candle (in actuality, a small puddle of long-melted wax) Sunny knelt at the edge of our rag-stuffed mattress shell and sat the pair of canteen cups in her right hand to the mattress beside me, then placed the bottle of amber-colored liquid in her left on the floor.

"Whiskey. . .Don't know what brand. The label's gone." She thumped the bottle's long neck with her forefinger. "Cosnetti and Asbury found a couple of cases buried in the rubble under what was once a pub." She popped the top and poured generous helpings in both cups. "It'd be nice if we had power for the refrigerator downstairs. . .for ice cubes."

"As long as we're wishing, a T-bone, medium-well, and a baked potato with sour cream and chives," I offered, decidedly sarcastic, throwing in a playful wink before reaching down to claim one of the cups.

There were few comforts in war. You took them as they came. And this one, I had to admit, came under the heading of compassionate god-send.

One of them, I should say. Sunny being the other.

Our gazes touched momentarily, following our initial sips, then dropped away. Mine to the revealing expanse of flesh visible between the halves of her fatigue blouse.

We had been comrades, then friends, for more than a decade; for at least a dozen campaigns, on both sides of the Atlantic. For the past 3 years, co-commanders of the Foxtrot Company, Second Platoon upper echelon, and though neither of us consciously realized it, inevitably, lovers.

"You think they know?" I asked. "About us, I mean."

"Our people might be combat worn, but they're not stupid. . .Or resentful. I can't speak for what they think about me, but they respect you. They would never begrudge you. . .*us* a little relief."

"Besides. . .and you didn't hear this from me," she added, winking back at me, "Alcohol wasn't the only thing Cosnetti's team found. A little camp on the edge of Grid 4. Five families of Roma. . .mothers, daughters, granddaughters, and no men over the age of seven. I sort of gave the boys the nod for a moonlight swap meet, so long as it didn't interfere with the perimeter guard and they kept the enthusiasm down to an occasional shriek."

"In any case," she added, "It's a better choice than having them exposed to one of the shipyard sleaze pits. It's bad enough their bodies are fighting off the fallout, but who knows how many flavors of STDs and radiated homemade booze those places foster."

"No problem. They earned it," I chuckled, finally sampling the contents of my cup.

"Oh, and by the way. . .Congrats," she raised her cup, toast-fashion. "I read the message from AI. . .*Colonel* Valiant."

I reciprocated her gesture. "And as my XO, that also bumps you up a step. So, back'atcha. . .Major Athena."

I cut myself off at that point, not wanting to piss on her parade. What appeared to be an 'attaboy' from The Powers That Be was more likely akin to giving the condemned prisoners a last meal before they slipped the noose around our necks.

Although it had been presented to the contrary, DragonFire had always been a shade short of a suicide mission. Especially now. . .going into the DC Sector—currently crawling with enemy elements—with less than half our support, labor, and materiel; locating, obtaining Protocol 45, the so-called 'War Ender,' then getting out to rendezvous with our Allied submarine off the Maryland coast. To be honest, the odds of survival were about the same as running through a cage-load of hungry lions in a pork chop overcoat.

Chapter 4
What's Past Is Prologue

Personal Journal
July 27, 2062
2210 hours
To whomever finds this journal, here is the story of how I came to be an IDF officer:

I had grown up among the ruins of Israel af-ter the Big Blast when China had decided to put its foot down on claiming Taiwan and lobbed several missiles onto the USS Colin Powell. It, in turn, launched an attack on the Xiamen naval base, which prompted China to dispatch nuclear warheads to Washington, DC. And the powers in DC answered with an attack of their own during the wait.

Once Hamas had heard the US was hit and probably incapacitated to the point where it wouldn't be concerned about Israel, they sent a barrage of several missiles to Israel from various sites. Our David's Sling defense system shot down most, but not all, of them. One of the mis-siles hit our newly built nuclear power plant, causing an explosion and sending plumes of radi-oactive material into the atmosphere. And that's when the remaining members of the General Staff retaliated, obliterating Lebanon, northern Jor-dan, and southern Syria. Egypt and Saudi Arabia were mostly unscathed, but wanting no parts of a war, sent diplomatic messages promising no unilateral attacks and denying involvement with Hamas or Hezbollah. Israel didn't believe them but had its plate full dealing with nuclear fallout. Since my father was an officer in the IDF, we had been living on base but were evacuated to a base farther away that had underground bunkers. We were sheltered from the worst of it, but the images from the news painted a grim picture. So many had died...and were dying.

For months, children never went outside; we had to content ourselves playing quietly with the few toys and games stored in the bunker. We began making up our own games like Radiation Monster and Exposure Time. We tried to ignore the hushed voices and silent tears, the sudden turning away accompanied by soft sobs. The parents tried to make things cheerful as best they could, even over Purim and Pessah (Passover). But instead of burning forbidden foodstuffs (foods with leaven), we hid them under a tarpaulin until Passover ended.

Many months passed before we were allowed out, thanks to the air scrubbers, and we moved into a vacated home of someone who had been in Jordan when the bombs dropped. At least that's what we were told. Bombs had been dropped in other parts of the world, as well, setting nation against nation. The UK, USA, France, and Germany decided on an alliance and had invited Israel. But we had decided to join on a case-by-case basis, seeking collaboration on efforts where our interests were served, and bowing out if they were not.

Children had still gone to school to try to resume a semblance of normalcy, but classes were frequently interrupted with radiation-level warnings, depending on wind direction and speed, and we would be hurried to the bunkers. But there were reports of mutations among animals and some newborns. Over the years, we tried to live as normally as we did before the Blast—observing Jewish holidays, going to dances, dating—but the tension of death always lingered in the background, tainting both our society and our relationships with each other.

When I turned 18, I received my Tzav Rishon, or First Calling, from the military, to report for a day-long exam and interview. I bade farewell to my parents and reported for Tironut (basic training).

#

Seren Zana Shalom's Tent
July 27, 2062
0142 hours

I awoke from a light sleep with green blinking in my periphery . . . an incoming message on my personal comm. I tapped my temple to open it. Incoming message:

> Blue Team observed a team of three mercbots. They were damaged and trying to use each other's parts to make two whole ones. Destroyed on site. Be on the lookout for more.
>
> End message.

"Shit." *They're getting smarter.*

Mercbots had been numerous at the start of the war, each army having their own version, rolling up on groups of soldiers as 6-inch balls of steel, then lengthening to 3 feet of swirling razors, edges sharp enough to slice bone. Victims had been carried into Medical with various body parts cut to pulp. Israel had invented a detection program based on their minute acoustic signatures for each type, and had destroyed many of them, but if the signatures changed, then we would have to start over on countermeasures. Another thing to worry about.

"Relay to rest of the platoon. Send remnants to Tech for analysis. Shalom out."

Chapter 5
Faith is Just Another Word for Nothing Left to Lose

Commander's Journal
July 28, 2062
0235 hours
It's quiet now, but Listening Post Charlie radioed a sitrep to the sentries on our Southeastern perimeter of gunfire and explosions coming from deep within the DC Capitol sector. Not that it was entirely necessary. Nor was it entirely unexpected. First, earlier reports from our deep recon team identified a number of populated areas within and around the city. And secondly, sound waves carry farther at night and I am a light sleeper. Athena and I were both aroused into wakefulness by the distant staccato crackle and intermittent thump of what was obviously a raging fire fight. As to who, why, and its implications concerning our own assignment. . .questions yet to be answered.

#

Commander's Journal
July 28, 2062
1330 hours
An unexpected development. Somehow—a miracle, if I believed in such things—a single

squad managed to survive the Canadian attacks on Foxtrot Company and catch up with us. We now have a group of seven men added to our contingent of twenty-five, an armored personnel vehicle, and sorely needed weapons. Unfortunately, the supplies they brought with them were barely enough to sustain their own forces, leaving us only slightly better equipped than we were before their arrival.

Ammunition, weapons, and manpower, however, are not our most crucial concerns. Ration stores were already low prior to the arrival of the Fourth Platoon's survivors and with those additional mouths to feed, I estimate that our food-stuffs will be depleted in less than two weeks. Also, most recent inventory and reports from the group medical officer—due to theft by deserters—show significant shortages in sterile bandages, blood plasma, morphine, KI-9, potassium iodide, and radiation pills. The pills being the most critical item of all.

Although, for the record, she has given me all the credit, it was Sunny's idea to move the Roma community into our base camp. It made sense, she said, for a number of reasons. The first being the issue of their vulnerability (and ours) because of their proximity to us. Although the lion's share of legitimate threats—actual military factions— are spread out in a wide arc in our foreground, our patrols have found scattered signs of the presence of Red Dogs, outlaw raiders made up of military deserters, former gang bangers, and ex-

soldiers from defunct Mafia and drug cartels who prey upon unprotected civilians.

Secondly, bringing the Roma into our camp prevented a hostile force from gaining a foothold in an area that would compromise our safety.

Third, and on a more personal note, group morale. For most of the unit, Sunny and I in-cluded, it has been a long while. . .years, in fact, since they experienced the atmosphere of commu-nity. The sights and sounds of family units, chil-dren at play, frequent smiles and the looks of appreciation and gratitude—things we had all become accustomed to and took for granted in the days before the world was snatched into mad-ness.

"Notice the difference. . .*sir?*" Sunny queried softly, adding a playful verbal poke as we neared the conclusion of our daily walking tour of the now-extended camp.

"The camp. . .More people than there were yesterday," I answered, semi-facetious, to be sure. I knew, of course, where her question was headed. And, knowing her as I did, I knew that I was being set up for one of Sunny's involved and in-depth observations.

"I'm going to assume you also notice how that affects our people," she said. "They're a lot happier. . .emotionally stable. A few hours ago, it wouldn't have taken much for most, if not all of them, to go over the wall. But then, I'm pretty sure I'm not telling you anything you haven't been thinking lately."

"It's crossed my mind once or twice," I acknowledged, leaving out the part where, for one, I wouldn't have blamed them and, for another, I seriously considered joining them.

We stopped for a moment at the inner rim of the Roma encampment and watched as Mahala, the tribe's Queen, spoke to a gathering of young women in a lean-to attached to her horse-driven RV.

"She is one of the strongest women I have ever met," Sunny resumed when we started to walk again. "There were two tribes when they first started out from Wyoming—almost 300 people. Two years of attacks by raiders and rape gangs, the murders of their husbands, sons, fathers, and siblings, brutal weather, fallout rain. . .things that would have driven weaker spirits to lay down and give up. But they didn't. . .they never surrendered. Never stopped. That is a determination our people need. Especially now."

"I know how you feel about this war," she continued. "I hate it, too. But if there is even the slightest chance we can find the thing that will end this insanity, then our mission is worth it. You just have to have a little faith."

Chapter 6
The Owl and the Pussycat

Commander's Journal
August 1, 2062
0530 hours
*Day 128. Finally, Sergeant **Absalom**'s deep recon/search team picked up an encrypted digital text burst, authenticated, from FireDrake. Unfortunately, sunrise is less than an hour away. Absalom's team is too deep inside the Hot Zone to make their way back to base camp without putting themselves at risk. Insofar as myself and Sunny are the only members of the mission who can decrypt the text burst, I'll have to wait at least another 15 hours before it's delivered. Providing, of course, Absalom and his team manage to return unscathed.*

#

Commander's Journal
August 1, 2062
2200 hours

The decrypted text burst from FireDrake was simple. It read: INDEPENDENT POWER SIGNATURE DETECTED – TUNNEL COMPLEX BENEATH THE WHITE HOUSE – LOCATION OF PROTOCOL 45 A 99.98% PROBABILITY – AWAIT YOUR ORDERS TO PROCEED. Good news? Of a fashion. What concerns me more is the contents of Sergeant Absalom's report on enemy identification and their movement in and around the DC corridor.

ROKs, North Korean Marines, Chinese SOF – Special Ops Forces, Russian Spetsnaz, the New IRA, and November Dawn. In Absalom's words, Heavy hitters all, like army ants looking for a picnic. And I have a feeling we're it.

#

"You've been quiet, ValJean," Sunny said, moving close to massage the nape of my neck. "You haven't said a word since Herschel's debriefing."

True enough, I had neither spoken, nor moved, from the window overlooking the courtyard encampment since the end of Sergeant Absalom's delivery of FireDrake's coded message and the verbal and the visual drone-recorded intel of the activities in the Hot Zone. The truth is, I couldn't. Didn't want to. And probably wouldn't have for. . .who knows how long if Sunny hadn't broken the paralyzing grip of my dark ruminations.

Of course, her use of my birth name helped.

"Do you believe in omens?" I asked, turning to look at her. My gaze was still not quite focused in the here and now. "Signs, warnings of things that. . .could happen?"

"Are we talking ESP? Voices from God and the Great Beyond?" Sunny's response was blatantly flippant. For a moment or so, at any rate. "Okay. All right," she said, semi-apologetic. "I believe in instinct. I believe that, based on training, experience, and prevailing circumstances, our minds can make certain assumptions. Otherwise, I'd have to say. . .No."

"I didn't, either. But my grandmother, Nana Sue, did. She believed that certain birds—ravens and owls—were omens of death."

She didn't laugh, but I could sense it, held in check at the back of her throat. "Birds?"

"Owls, to be on point," I clarified. "And bear with me before you start to wonder if I'm slipping into cuckoo land."

I led her away from the window, then back to the makeshift table designated 'the Ops Center' and the battery-powered MKV-97, the digital optical pak used to view recorded footage from the recon team's stealth drone.

Sunny stood patiently while the screen images moved over scenes of crumbled, bombed-out ruins, potholed streets, and sporadic groups of bedraggled city dwellers. "There," I finally announced and tapped the PAUSE button to freeze the image of the staircase leading up to the Lincoln Memorial.

"And I'm looking at. . .?" Sunny prompted.

I tapped the ZOOM IN function, zeroing in on a small, dark smudge at the top of the stairs.

An owl.

"Don't ask me what type," I said before she could respond. "But I've got a question for you. . .Since we crossed over from Canada——and not counting Mahala's horses——what's the largest, and most prevalent animal or insect you've seen?"

I cut her off again. "I'll answer for you. Besides the mutated wolves we ran into in Canada, the fallout has pretty much wiped out most of the lower forms, with the exceptions of rats and cockroaches. So, disregarding the fact that we're in the city, where did that owl come from?"

I gave her a moment or so to mull it over before I continued. "An owl just like the one that landed on top of Mahala's RV a half hour ago, by the way."

"Coincidence?" she replied.

"I would accept that, at any other time," I said, unfreezing the image and allowing the visuals to continue, though at a slightly accelerated speed.

The drone slowed and finally hovered over a noticeably cleared cul-de-sac, darkened save for an awning-capped storefront whose pitted walkway was lined on both sides with ground-mounted torches. At the top of its tattered and discolored awning was a sign that featured the image of a pink feline—a pussycat.

The drone's camera paused a few seconds, zooming in on a cluster of figures below the awning, three women and four men. One of the men the camera found particularly interesting. He stood in partial profile, his features blocked, from the jawline up, by the awning's front flap and covered on at least three sides by the trio of near-nude women.

"I noticed something the first time we watched the footage," I told her, and tapped the PAUSE again. "Tell me what you see."

"And besides the obvious," I threw in.

Sunny's response came within seconds. "The man, the one the women are crawling over," the disgust in her tone prompted a quick grin, "He's not a local. In fact, the way he's dressed says he isn't even a native of the area. . .even he tries to pass himself off as such——baggy, ill-fitting clothes. But. . ." She paused, giving me a quick cognizant glance. "But his footwear. . .those are. . .military-issue combat boots."

"They are, indeed. Now check out his forearm. The one curved around the blonde's hip. What do you see?"

"It looks like a tattoo."

"It is. And look close. . .A tattoo of what?"

Sunny leaned closer to the screen, squinting as she studied the slightly hazy image. "Some kind of bird," she spoke after a moment, then jerked upright as recognition kicked in. "It's an——"

"Owl," I cut in. "A sports club tat, to be exact. For a semi-pro baseball team. . .The Black Oak Owls from Black Oak, Arkansas. The hometown and the former ball team of a certain squad leader. Hell, he's bragged about it enough since the day he first transferred in."

"Green, Third Squad," Sunny chimed in. "What the hell is that son-of-a-bitch doing so deep in the Hot Zone?"

"I'd say that's obvious, too. . .At least at face value," I said. "But that's not the question. . .questions-plural, we should be asking."

I switched off the device and returned to the window, with Sunny attentively on my heels.

"What else was he doing there?" Sunny said.

"That's one. And probably the most important," I replied. "One we had better find the answer to as soon as possible."

Omens. Whether or not, like my Nana Sue, I believe in the traditional meaning of the term was moot. One thing was certain: something out there was definitely throwing us a warning.

#

Seren Zana Shalom's Tent
August 2, 2062
0730 hours

"Rav Nagad Reisen, please come to my tent." I clicked off my comm. After a few minutes, he strode up to my tent flap wearing a wry smile. Reisen was tall and had a general devil-may-care attitude but was a whiz at consolidating disparate information into a cohesive narrative. If I wasn't afraid of losing my unit's respect, I would have visited his tent on numerous occasions. Perhaps after the war…

"You wanted me, ma'am?"

I adopted a stern posture. "What's the latest?"

"The US Second Platoon received an encrypted message around 22 hours last night. We're still trying to decrypt.

"Tech reassembled the mercbots but they want one that's intact in order to test it.

41

"And Second Platoon are still in Georgetown and Barney Circle, shoring up forces at Bolling Air Base and the Navy Yard. They took in a group of Roma, mostly women and children, but effectively taking a potential player off the board. The Red Dogs are keeping silent, watching, but conducting business among the civilians, mostly in Trinidad. The ROKs have taken and are holding Greenway and Fort Dupont just over the Anacostia. The Chinese have moved into Chinatown and Judiciary Square. The Spetsnaz are downtown and at Foggy Bottom, and the New IRA are in the Arboretum and Ivy City. In other words, we're surrounded by adversarial forces."

I scoffed. "When are we not?" We were hunkered down among the ruins of bombed-out houses and their dirt-packed back yards. We'd built a perimeter around the main area, trying to give ourselves some semblance of security, but we all knew that if hit with enough firepower, the corrugated metal walls would fall down like Jericho.

"Tell the teams to try and capture a mercbot without blowing it to bits first. Any movement?"

"No, but the tension's so thick, you could eat it for lunch. Everyone's waiting for something to pop off. If it does, it's gonna be…" He trailed off, leaving the thought lingering between us.

A full-on slaughter, I thought, but didn't voice. Morale was on life support. "Who's the weakest link in the Second Platoon?" I bit my lip as I paced the floor, thinking.

"One Staff Sergeant Dale Green. He sneaks off guard duty at least twice a week to visit the local women and returns drunk. Sober enough to walk, but not enough to fend off a fight."

"Excellent. Send me his schedule and a picture."

Reisen's smile widened. "You doing a little recon of your own?"

"I'm not ex-Mossad for nothing."

"On it." Reisen tapped the tent pole twice and left.

#

The Mall
Washington, DC
August 1, 2230 hours
The Mall had once been an area ringed by Smithsonian museums and sandwiched between the US Capitol and the Lincoln Memorial. It was now populated with lean-to juke joints, bars, and whorehouses. But it had been deemed neutral territory by the factions occupying the area.

I sidled up to the door of a place named The Bar, trying not to pull my too-short skirt—made from old camouflage—farther down my thin legs. Broken glass glittered on top of the luminescent evercrete, which had once lit the way to more respectable establishments. Rats dashed among the shadows, and I felt a slight pang of pity for them, for there was little to be had except some diesel-engine gin and expired MREs. Old music blared out the broken windows...songs from the early 2030s. The stuff my parents used to listen to. We were all stuck in a nuclear limbo...no new movies or bands, recycled clothing, rusted cars. Whatever fun we had, we pretty much had to make it on our own.

I hazarded up the makeshift cardboard-and-wood steps and walked inside. The place was lit by a few candles and hurricane lamps. A long counter made of hammered corrugated aluminum lined one side of the room, fronted by a row of stools. A bartender stood behind the counter, pouring beige liquid from a tin pitcher into little tin cups. I paused as my eyes adjusted and I saw him. Staff Sergeant Dale Green. He was sitting at a table in the corner with a blonde drug addict grinding her bony ass into his crotch...only she didn't have any rhythm. He didn't look as if he was enjoying it much, but what else was there to do?

I ordered up two drinks and paid with a fresh MRE I'd stashed in my jacket, for which the bartender seemed grateful. Then I strode over to Green's table and caught the blonde's gaze.

"Scram."

She hesitated, a puzzled look on her face, until I put down the drinks and yanked her, sending her flying into the next table. Green mirrored her quizzical look until I handed him a drink. Then he smiled and patted his lap. I took the proffered seat and leaned in. He smelled of bootleg hooch and a year's worth of caked-on sweat. I cleared my throat and tried to ignore the stench, then rustled up a smile and loud whispered in his ear to be heard above the din.

"You're cute."

"Oh, yeah? I never seen you round here before."

"Then it's your lucky night." I giggled.

He downed his drink in one swallow. "Well, all right. What say we go upstairs, find us a room?"

He wasted no time. *Good.* I got up from his lap and took his hand. Led him to the back where the stairs hugged the far wall. They looked sturdier than the steps out front, but I tested each small landing before I put my full weight on it, which was hard to do with his hand grabbing my ass the whole way. He would definitely pay for that. After I reached the second floor, I jiggled the handles to the doors that lined the hallway. I found an empty room on my third try. He grabbed both my butt cheeks and I turned to face him as he closed the door behind him with his foot. The odor of mold and rotted wood permeated the room. I withdrew the hypo from my cleavage, bit off the cap, and jabbed him in the neck. His delayed reaction played on his face like a slow-motion horror flick...the wide eyes, the gaping mouth. The reflection from the blinking neon sign in the wall mirror. All we needed was a soundtrack.

"Relax, it's just a little something to loosen your tongue. You're not dying. Now, what are your platoon's orders?" I cradled his head as I lowered him slowly to the dirty mattress on the floor.

His eyes had a faraway look that briefly focused after blinking. "To stay in place until further orders."

"What recent satcom messages have you received?"

"I dunno. They're encrypted. We got one last night. The Colonel and his squeeze, Captain Athena, are the only ones who can decrypt."

"What do you know about Protocol 45?"

He shook his head. "Nothing confirmed. Just rumors that it's supposed to end the war. But no one knows what it is or where."

"What other news, what gossip have you heard?"

"We were supposed to meet up with Third Platoon, but they never made it. A squad from Foxtrot Company joined us. Seven troops. They brought an armored car and some food, but not enough."

"What's the status of your supplies?"

"Nearly gone. Six deserters took a large part of our rations. We're going to start eating each other soon."

There was fear in Dale's eyes, along with a resignation I had seen on the faces of the condemned. The war had pretty much stomped out anyone's hopes and dreams of a better tomorrow. I couldn't help but say, "It's going to be all right."

Loud voices sounded on the floor below, as if giving orders, then a few screams. I sprang to the window and looked out. An empty ROK truck was parked in front of the door, which meant they would be shooting their way into the room any moment. I kicked the area around the window until the wood splintered, and the window fell out. Grabbed the mattress and threw it outside, then hauled up Dale and chucked him after it. Since he was drunk, he landed limp, staring up at me as I dove toward him. I landed on top of him and rolled off, clutching his shirt as I moved. Yelling filled the room upstairs as bullets rained down, and I braced myself against the ROK truck as I threw Dale inside. I climbed in after, pushed the button to start, and threw it in drive as a shot ricocheted off the bumper. Grateful the ROK believed in bullet-proof armor, I tore off down the street, almost running over a couple of drunks by the side of the road. The ricocheting stopped and I slapped the comm on the back of my ear as I headed for Kingman Park.

"Shalom to Reisen! I'm coming in hot with the ROK on my ass. I need guns blazing as soon as you see them."

"Shit! On it!"

What the hell were the ROK doing at a run-down juke joint? If they had been keeping tabs on both me and Green, maybe they were trying to kill two birds with one stone. And speaking of Green, Second Platoon wouldn't be too happy their man was being driven to Israeli territory with the ROK likely close behind. I turned to look at Green, who was very quiet, even for someone under the influence. He sat slumped to his right, head resting against the window.

"Dale?" I clawed his shirt and came away with a wet hand. "Shit. Dale…Dale!"

I shook him, yelling his name, but no response came. He must have gotten hit after I rolled off of him. Second Platoon would kill me if I rolled up on their perimeter with a dead sergeant. My heart pounded in my chest and my breathing came in gulps.

Calm down. Don't panic. Think.

I had to get the truck off the street as soon as possible, so I kept off the main roads and wound through neighborhoods with the headlights off. It took me a half hour to make it back to Kingman Park, and by the time I got there, they were already involved in a firefight with the ROK.

Shit! That was ammo being wasted.

I wound around the back of the Park and commed Sergeant Goldberg to tell him it was me in the mysterious black truck that was coming up to the gate. He approached me cautiously, rifle raised, as I drove up, until I rolled down the window and offered a casual smile.

"Daaaamn, Captain. It *is* you. How'd you get a Korean truck? … And a…dead American?"

"Long story. Just open the gate. I need to hide this before our trigger-happy friends on the other end of the Park find out."

"Yes, ma'am. I heard fire and wanted to join but I was ordered to stay put."

"You saved *my* life, Goldberg. Thanks."

He smiled and waved me through the makeshift gate of soldered iron fencing, aluminum cans, corrugated sheet metal, and whatever else we could find to tack together a barricade. I drove the truck behind a tent and threw a tarp over it. I'd need time to figure out what to do with Dale's body.

"Sorry, Dale." His family, if he had any, should be notified of his passing, I thought.

A tall tree nearby provided a perfect vantage point, so I climbed it to assess the situation out front. Twenty or so ROK troops and four trucks were exchanging fire with thirty of our troops, but we had the advantage of a barricade. I remembered we still had three surface-to-air missiles so I climbed down and headed for the armory, figuring they could go in reverse. Air to surface.

After hauling the weapon up the tree, I looked through the scope and spied a line of sight that cleared my troops but would land in the middle of the melee on the other side of the fence.

I commed Reisen. "Shalom here. I'm about to shoot off a missile so order the troops back."

"Where the fuck are you? And where have you been?"

"I drove around back. I'm in the tree next to the canteen. You've got your orders, segen."

Reisen's voice sounded throughout the comm system ordering everyone to pull back. The Koreans made the mistake of thinking they were winning and tried to press an imagined advantage.

Once my troops had pulled back, I launched the missile, which shot out with a whoosh and a bang. It landed on an armored vehicle, obliterating it and the surrounding area for 40 feet. When the smoke cleared, a large crater marked the ground where the Korean soldiers had been. The pavement under the front gate had crumbled. We would have to shore that up. I doubted the ROK wanted to get into an all-out battle over a stolen truck and would think twice about sending more men, but still, I would give the order to triple the patrol. No one was going to get any sleep for a long time.

Chapter 7
And the Beat Goes On

OUT: Satellite Communiqué

AUTH.CODE: Allied Command – Camelot

ENCRYPTION PROTOCOL: Lexicon 4 – Excalibur

STATUS: Most Urgent

FROM: Valiant, Colonel, Commander Operation DragonFire

TO: Mercury, Major, Camelot – AI-7, ALLIED INTELLIGENCE

Message As Follows –

Item 1 – Possibility of traitor in the ranks. Type and extent of leak information unknown.

Item 2 – Query: Proceed or Abort Mission.

Item 3 – Query: Actions as to Subject, Item 1.

PLEASE ADVISE.

Message Ends.

INCOMING: Satellite Communiqué

AUTH.CODE: Allied Command – Camelot

ENCRYPTION PROTOCOL: Lexicon 4 – Excalibur

DOWNLOAD/RECORD: Active

FROM: Mercury, Major, Camelot – AI-7, ALLIED INTELLIGENCE

TO: Valiant, Colonel, Commander Operation DragonFire

Dispatch As Follows –

RESPONSE TO - Item 1 – Acknowledged.

RESPONSE TO - Item 2 – Mission Proceeds as per orders. DO NOT, Repeat DO NOT ABORT.

RESPONSE TO - Item 3 – Investigate extent of compromised information. ACTION: Sanitize.

Dispatch Ends.

Commander's Journal
August 2, 2062
0800 hours

Can't say I was surprised by the response from Command. Especially from AI. They are spooks, after all. A side of Allied Command populated by people who see the world only in black and white.

Regardless of what Sergeant Green may or may not have done, it still pains me that, in keeping with protocol, I have to treat him as a threat to the mission and the safety of the unit. The other squad leaders have been covertly briefed on the situation and advised to keep close watch on Sergeant Green, reporting his ongoing activities to either myself or Major Athena.

In light of the situation—as well as recent reports from deep recon and our advance element—I have put the unit on alert. At 0400 hours, we contact the advance agent and set up a rendezvous. We move out, into the Hot Zone, to kick off Operation DragonFire at 0530.

#

Segen Bichler's Tent
August 2, 2062
0900 hours

I strode into Bichler's tent and leveled a gaze at him, hands on my hips. I doubt anyone had gotten any sleep the previous night as we waited on more Koreans to show up. But we hadn't heard anything more from the ROK, so that was a plus. I was desperately trying to find the shiny lining.

"Well, last night was a shitshow." Bichler ran his hand through his hair. "Tell me you at least got something from the dead American that's sitting in a ROK truck on our base."

I shook my head. "Nothing much. Green was a grunt. Said only the platoon leader and his girl-friend could decrypt messages. Didn't know what Protocol 45 was. They met up with another pla-toon and gained seven men but lost six troops as deserters, who stole a large amount of food."

"Maybe we can starve them out?"

"That would take too long, and us along with it. What about Tech?"

"Oh, right." Bichler snapped his fingers. "They figured out the mercbots' new acoustic signatures AND…learned how to hijack their sig-nal. We can make them do what we want."

I sighed in relief. "Some good news for once. What about the encrypted message? Have they made any headway?"

"Haven't heard anything more. Sorry."

As if on cue, Mizrahi appeared in the tent flap, sweat staining his armpits. "Seren, we decrypted part of Second Platoon's message. All we could get was Tunnel and 45."

My heart leaped. "Forty-five? That's got to be Protocol 45." *Finally.* "And tunnel?" My mind raced. "Recon has maps of underground areas?"

"Yeah, one of the first things on their list when we get to a new area."

"Well, get them here now. I have a feeling we don't have much time."

Seren Shalom's Tent
August 2, 2062
1305 hours

Segen Omer swept into my tent with the swagger of a conquering Roman, reveling in the attention the recon teams were paying him. I considered having someone else give the briefing, but he was the most knowledgeable and the teams' leader.

After the twenty-five of us who had crammed into my tent quieted down, Omer accessed our intranet from his watch band and spooled up a map of DC with its tunnels marked in red. It hovered over the table like a piece of nonfungible art.

"DC has a veritable underground city. And our robotic snakes have mapped 90 percent of them. There are tunnels crisscrossing the Capitol building, the White House, and the Monument, not to mention the subway lines. Trying to find P45 in these tunnels would be like finding a virgin in the IDF." A round of laughter.

I leaned forward from the opposite end of the table. "Which are the most heavily fortified?"

"The ones under the White House, naturally."

I nodded. "Then that's where we'll go. I want your teams to write up battle strategies for a push toward the White House, for deployment first thing in the morning. I don't know what the other factions know about this but assume the worst. Lord willing, we'll be pleasantly surprised tomorrow, but if not, we can at least be ready. And put some more drones on Second Platoon. I want to know what they're up to."

As the teams started filing out, I said a silent prayer in the name of my new God.

Segen Omer's Tent
August 3, 2062
0314 hours
"Heads up."

I stood behind Omer's chair sipping on my second cup of coffee as the blended images of fifty drone dragonflies coalesced above Omer's desk. They used a synthetic aperture sensor, a radar system that produced high-res images. Second Platoon was gassing up vehicles and gathering weapons and ammo. I pointed at a vehicle to the right of center.

"Look, they still have modular hybrid UGVs. Most of them got blown up by mercbots at the start of the war."

"I guess they figure the bots are gone so why not."

"Only we've got a surprise for them on that front." I gulped down the last bit of my drink and tossed the tin cup into Omer's makeshift sink. "We need to follow them. They apparently have more intel than us on P45. Get your teams ready."

Omer stood up and pushed the chair out of the way so he could stand nose-to-nose with me.

"And how do we know they're not putting on a show for us right now, making it look like they're heading out one way when in actuality, their recon teams are heading someplace else?"

I squared my shoulders and lifted my chin. I recognized that look, the fixed gaze, set mouth, and hot breath. Seen it from my first day in the army. Felt it suddenly boiling off men…off him, like stench from shit. Like a switch turned on…just like that.

"Because it's too late in the game for bullshit. Second Platoon just got orders. They're moving out for the final push. So stop dicking around and carry out your orders."

"Look around. The world's falling apart. Why should I keep taking orders from you? A woman. And a Black one at that."

And there it was. I knew it'd been there all along, simmering—seething—waiting for a catalyst.

Omer was serving in the Nahal Haredi program that catered to religious proscriptions regarding food, prayer, ban on contact with women, and the like. It had been easier to maintain in Israel, but in the field, with fewer soldiers to do the work and even fewer resources to go around, those commandments and food proscriptions had pretty much gone out the window. I'd seen Orthodox soldiers bite the head off a rabbit and suck out the blood in extreme conditions. But the beliefs…the chauvinism…those stayed.

But I'd worked out a system. I pressed the internal comm behind my ear. "Seren Bichler, Top Care."

"Shit…on it," came the reply.

Omer advanced as I backed away. "Your little minion can't help you. My men follow me."

He grabbed my left arm and dug the tips of his fingers into my triceps. I fisted him in the throat, hard. Twice. I'd practiced. He gasped and stumbled backward, clutching his neck.

Bichler ran into the tent, followed by two guards. He stopped short and looked up at me.

"Stick his ass in the hole and post a guard. We're moving out."

Chapter 8
All the King's Horses

Commander's Journal
August 3, 2062
0425 hours
Day 130. This will be my last entry until (hopefully) the end of the mission and our successful rendezvous/extraction. Though I'm not kidding myself. It could very well be the last before I show up in the Afterlife. Still, in the words of my ever-optimistic XO, 'Positive thoughts, positive outcome.'

*It's quiet now. Deathly quiet—literally. But the memories of the **past few** hours still thunder a hellish cacophony in my thoughts.*

I had no illusions as to what we were facing, moving toward the heart of the Capitol. Inasmuch as, first of all, there was no doubt whatsoever that all of the opposing forces therein were as aware of our presence as we were of theirs. And, of course, there was the unsettling element of uncertainty, of stomach-churning anxiety concerning what our suspected traitor, Dale Green, may have revealed to the enemy regarding our strengths, weaknesses, et cetera. A situation made all the more alarming by the fact that, as of 0500 hours, Staff Sergeant Green failed to report for duty and has since been listed as AWOL—

Absent Without Leave. At this point, I'd say Missing in Action is a more accurate assumption.

Secondly, with stealth also being out of the question, our one strategic advantage was that the city's occupying forces would be off guard by our arrival and have little or no time to set up an organized defense. To that end, for the Operation designated Dark Equus, our forces were divided into four groups.

Queen's Mare, led by Major Athena, was to enter the district first. They would make contact with the Advance Team, receive the intel on the probable location, and transmit that intel to me. As it turned out, that location was, of all places, the White House.

How's that for irony.

Teams Mustang Beta and Charlie were to move parallel to our position, two klicks to our left and right flanks as a guard and deterrent against ambushes and delaying actions, while Queen's Mare swung in to secure our rear.

Meanwhile myself, King's Stallion, along with the APC and the late-comers from Foxtrot Company, would make a head-on run—a suicide run—for the White House in the hopes of securing a beachhead, if you will. . .an entrenched and defended position from which we could continue the search for Protocol 45.

Sadly, things didn't quite work out that way.

Chapter 9
All the King's Men

Second Platoon

"Queen's Mare to King's Stallion. Contact. I say again, *Contact!*" Even without the affirming trigger word, it was Athena's tone—the alarm; the urgency, the barely contained terror—that made her ensuing report almost unnecessary. "Under heavy fire. Mortar barrage and small arms from both flanks."

And before I could respond, "Mustang Charlie to King's Stallion. Contact, Northwest sector. Automatic weapons fire has us pinned down. I repeat, pinned down, unable to move—over."

"King's Stallion to all Teams. Stand by. . .I repeat, stand by," I answered, then tapped the helmet of the APC's driver to indicate that I needed the vehicle to stop. I signaled the driver with a swiping motion across my throat to show, also, I wanted him to shut off the engine, hoping against hope that the premonition that suddenly sprouted within me proved no more than cautious paranoia.

It didn't.

The APC's V6 diesel engine's rumbling growl had no more than ebbed to a series of sporadic clicks when, even through the vehicle's thick armor-plated hull, my ears picked up the distant but undeniable chaotic roll of explosive thunder and the fireworks-like pop of small arms fire. . .from all directions, it seemed.

Dammit! Our opposing forces weren't as unprepared as I'd calculated and it appeared we had walked into, coordinated or separately advantageous, a series of mass ambushes.

My hands shook as I keyed the APC's radio-to-helmet commlink. "Stallion to all teams. Break off all contact. I say again, break contact, lay down suppressing fire and fall back to main column, over."

"Negative, Stallion." Athena was the first to respond. "Attacking forces too severe. We are cut off. . .all avenues blocked. We are pinned down, over."

Teams Charlie and Beta keyed in moments later with similar reports, all of them pinned down and close to being overwhelmed.

At that point, with no resistance or countering fire forward of our position, there was only one clear option—to continue our run for the White House and hope that, somehow, the others would survive to reinforce and support us.

That was four hours ago. Three hours forty-five minutes since our own inevitable clash with several unidentified units along Pennsylvania Avenue; since an RPG strike took out the APC's left track (and mortally wounded its driver); and those of us who survived were forced to battle our way—inch by bloody inch—on foot the last few blocks toward, and into the overgrown, war-torn area that was once the White House South Lawn.

Chapter 10
Us and Them aka Come Rain or Come Shine

IDF

The rain came down in torrents—the last gasps of Earth shrugging off humanity, I thought. We deserved it. Between the tons of CO_2, pollution, and radiation in the air; space debris in orbit; nations fighting nations; and chemicals in the water, we were pretty much done for. Most thought it would take a miracle to save us…which was why people were desperate for that elusive P45. But I knew the hard-bitten determination of mankind to survive would overcome in the end…even if there were only a few hundred of us left. It had happened before, 70,000 or so years ago. Whether I would be one of the lucky few this time around was purely speculative.

I was hunkered down with Green and Gold Teams under camo tarps with an armored transport vehicle, a sack of modified merc bots, and the remote to a temporarily downed swarm of drone dragonflies. I commed Reisen, the new Recon leader.

"Report."

His voice sounded in my head. "Weather's supposed to break in an hour. The major factions are pinned down in position. What are your orders?"

"Wait out the rain and send out the ground drones and snakes. I'm not stepping into a firefight if I can hang back and observe."

"What if someone else gets P45?"

"Then we'll just have to take it from them. Shalom out."

A low hum filled the air, as if carried along on a hot breeze that made you wish for stillness. The hum rose, like a buried giant from the earth. I turned to Bichler, whose face contorted into fearful recognition. Distant gunshots rang out above the hum and we both realized it at the same time. He spoke first.

"A swarm of gun-firing drones? In this weather?"

"Get in the car."

I flung open the hatch and waved everyone in before climbing in and yanking the hatch shut. Bullets ricocheted off the armor as soon as we were all inside. I expected the swarm to pass and with it, the sound of metal hitting metal, but it became louder and faster. I squeezed past Greenburg and scrambled into the driver's seat. The enclosed space smelled of sweat and must, but my nose quickly grew accustomed.

"Let's get the hell out of here. Someone's trying to push us along."

"Who?" The quizzical look on Greenburg's face matched his tone.

The Namer III roared to life and I eased it out from under the tarps, then pushed it to the max. It heaved like a hippo at dinner.

"A new player. The other factions' drones each number twenty at best. This?" I pointed skyward. "Two hundred, at least."

"Where are we going?"

"The White House. We'll pick up New York from Fourteenth Street and roll through the bombed-out Treasury Department to the South Lawn."

I rolled along Fourteenth, veering around large holes and abandoned cars. The gunshots ceased as I turned right onto New York Avenue, along with the rain. "Reisen was right. Weather's clearing. Send up the air drones. Let's get a read on what's going on out there."

Bichler grinned. "Yes, ma'am."

He patched through the grid of images onto the vehicle's display.

"Well?"

"Give me a minute. I can't assess 20 images in a few seconds."

I trundled onto the ruins of the Treasury Department and stopped. The once-distant sound of gunfire and explosions had drawn nearer and with it, a feeling of foreboding. We'd all known going in what our fates could be, but when faced with the inevitable, you never knew how you'd react. Greenburg was in the back making stupid jokes while the others replied with nervous laughter. Bichler was laser-focused on the images display, offering up a play-by-play rundown. And

I was determined to face down the source of the supposed doom and at least give as good as I got.

"Second Platoon is split, with one team headed for the White House, two teams flanking, and one advance team. They're all pinned under heavy fire from all the players, Spetsnaz, ROK, Chinese, Japanese, all in the Northwest sector." Greenburg pointed to each image as he spoke.

"It's decidedly quieter here in the Eastern sector, although that may change at any moment. And I trust the Americans more than the others. Send out the mercbots, camo covering. Program them to take out the non-American forces. Connect with Reisen." I hoped he hadn't run into heavy fire.

As if on cue, Reisen commed in. "Black Team to Judge Deborah."

I prayed for good news.

"Judge Deborah here."

"We've hacked everyone's comms and weapons systems, including Second Platoon's."

A feeling of elation swept away the foreboding, at least temporarily. "I love you."

A surprised "Oh!" came the reply.

"Confuse their systems, get them to fire on one another, everyone except the Americans. And open a link to Second Platoon. It's time we formally met our supposed ally."

#

Second Platoon

Sunshine and one hellacious rainstorm the past hour and change.

Too Old To Dance . . .

What was it they used to say, back when I was a kid? Rain when the sun shined meant the Devil was beating his wife. It always creeped me out, first of all, that someone supposedly as evil as Satan could have a wife. And, secondly, why the sun would shine on a situation like that.

As for the current situation, if anyone was getting a beating it was us—myself, my people (those of us left, at least), and the others. . .the enemy. Showered with droplets from an atmosphere saturated with the residual traces of radiation from the initial detonations of the first missile launches.

It was like that everywhere the past 10 years or so. Freakish weather patterns. Blizzards in South America, tornadoes in New York City, scorching heat waves in Alaska and the UK of up to 130° Fahrenheit, and torrential showers from near-cloudless skies. According to scientists, meteorologists, environmentalists, and such——back when television and radio networks still existed to allow their reports——it was because the number of near-simultaneous nuclear detonations, both atmospheric and ground level, had caused a slight but significant shift in the Earth's rotation. Which, as it turned out, also severely impacted certain tectonic plates and was the reason that, due to massive seismic eruptions, Japan was less than one-third its original size and there was a large sea-soaked island between San Francisco and Los Angeles.

Exposure to fallout and being soaked to the bone notwithstanding, there was a slight but grateful upside to the current situation. The rain coming down in sheets made any and/or all aggressive actions between our enemies and ourselves pretty much impossible. It's not easy to fight someone, let alone kill them, when you can barely see what you're firing at.

If little else, it gave us time to rest, to get our emotional bearings.

Seven of us evacuated the immobilized APC and made our run to the White House. Five by the time we reached the inner perimeter of the South Lawn. *God, I can still hear the screams and smell the stench of burning flesh from Privates Jefferson and Klein who were caught in the open by a flamethrower from the roof of a building less than 15 feet from our destination.*

And was that Asian I heard over the sounds of accompanying gunfire? A growling, guttural voice barking commands in Chinese? Korean? I'm no expert, and it's hard to tell in the heat of battle. But my recon teams have reported the presence of elements from the Chinese Red Storm and North Korean Marines. And I, myself, have seen bodies (or at least pieces and fragments of. . .) whose burned and/or blood-soaked uniforms carried the insignia of the JSDF, the Japan Self Defense Forces. . .Supposedly our allies.

Not surprising. This thing, Protocol 45, was as much a political as a military prize, or so I was previously briefed. If it was, indeed, the tool that would bring about the end of the war, *he, she, they* who possessed it would sit on the top of the heap in the political arena, bargaining-wise, once the shooting stopped.

What that meant for people like me—*grunts,* regular G.I.'s who fought their way through hell and shit and blood to get it—was a thing most probably as questionable, and as unpredictable, as the weather.

Speaking of which, it'd been almost a half hour now since the rain ceased. There were four of us an hour or so before the cloudburst; before our play to reach what appeared to be a massive hole in the South Wing that encompassed both the ground floor and second floor levels. A move, unfortunately, that was anticipated, intercepted, and blocked by a machine gun nest that ulti-mately took the life of Corporal Dolores Ruiz, but left Corporal Gary Tucker relatively un-scathed. A nest that was itself taken out, minutes later, by an RPG strike.

Definitely worth a prayer of Thanks to the Al-mighty, and to our saviors on the other side— whether saving our bacon was intended or not.

Bringing the count of Team King's Stallion down to three. Or so I thought.

Private Peterson and our comm tech, Private Deegle, weighed the importance of the mission against their survival and decided in favor of the latter. Both, it seemed, had used the rainstorm as cover for deserting their posts.

Did I blame them? Not really. To be honest, I'd be lying if I said I hadn't seriously considered aborting the mission, at least a dozen times long before we ventured into the city.

I gave them both credit for ingenuity, Deegle especially, for pulling their vanishing act with me being barely 5 feet away from them during the entire storm. If little else, in his defense, he'd at least had the courtesy to leave me the SatComm rig.

What that meant to the continuation (or the termination) of the mission, believe me, was something I thought long and strong about. I had no illusions as to what my life would be like if I chose the latter. A deserter, a disgraced officer, a fugitive forever on the run. On the other end, a single soldier, against unknown numbers, opposition-wise. . .The odds against success, against my survival, were less than encouraging.

My ultimate decision? I had to try. Better to die with honor than live under a dark cloud of shame.

During the storm, there had been occasional eruptions of gunfire, in the distance, all around us. There were still players in the game. And who knew. . .maybe some of them were mine.

I keyed the radio's mike three times, per protocol, as an identifier. "King's Stallion to all teams still active. I repeat, if still active, please respond, over."

There was a moment. . .long silence before a sudden burst of choppy static. Followed by. . .

"King's Stallion, this is Judge Deborah," an unexpected voice, definitely female, crackled over my earpiece. "I think maybe you and I should talk."

Chapter 11
We Are Soldiers

Second Platoon

All right. So somehow, someone managed to tap into our coded satellite comm frequency. That told me at least one thing. Insofar as, first of all, I could detect only a slight accent—second, an accent that was neither Middle Eastern, Slavic, or Asian—I was dealing with a major player. The Red Dog outlaw units didn't have the tech savvy. Nor did the local neighborhood defense groups. At least by most recent intel.

That left only one question. Actually two: Who? And what was their agenda?

And, like it or not, there was only one way to answer both.

"Moving kinda fast, aren't we, Judge Deborah?" I answered. "Right to third base on the first date. Current circumstances being what they are, dinner and a movie is out of the question. So... how about a little foreplay first? Like. . .who the fuck are you?"

"How bout," the voice responded after a short pause, "A Daughter of Israel?"

I gave it a lengthy beat before responding, more out of curiosity than strategy. "Israel. . .November Dawn? Last reports put you and yours somewhere in Greece. . .the Crete Islands—— over."

"Speaking on good authority," her reply came immediately, "as of six months past, Greece is now flying the colors of the China-Russian Coalition. A long and nasty fight, but they had the resources to persevere—over."

"Doesn't explain what brought you here. Or why I'm in your sights. Last I heard, Israel was an ally—over."

"On an as-needed basis. Israel survives," she answered. "And, like you, I am a soldier. I have my orders. And my mission. . .Protocol 45—over."

"Then I guess foreplay is finished," I said, "So, do we take this dance to the next stage or. . .what?"

Chapter 12
Yanking the Crank

Commander's Journal
August 4, 2062
0045 hours

Day 131. Seems circumstances have left me with more time than I originally calculated. Enough for at least another journal entry.

First – Insofar as I have received no responses from any of my units in more than 8 hours, I have to assume that they are either dead or physically unable to respond to my communications. I doubt very strongly that, under the conditions of our mission, they would be taken prisoner.

APP ALERT: As per protocol, I have uploaded a digital file with the names, ranks, and training profiles of every member of this command and mission. Let it be known, here, that they served with distinction and honor.

#

"The next stage," my adversary replied after a lengthy pause. "If by that you mean that you surrender to my forces. I give you my word you will be well treated."

Laughter. Actually, closer to an incredulous chuckle.

Was she serious? More to the point, did she seriously believe I was stupid enough to take her offer seriously? More than likely, she was fishing—feeling me out, testing the waters. Like myself, she was in the dark as to my resources—manpower and fire power—and, if not, we would still be trading bullets rather than words on our respective comm devices long before now.

"Very gracious of you, Judge," I called back. "But I'm afraid we must decline" . . .putting careful emphasis on the *we*. "My comrades and I are very comfortable with things as they are, thank you very much."

"Comrades." Her immediate response, and its accompanying (mocking) laughter was, admittedly, like a pin prick to the balloon of my already shrinking fortitude. "I doubt whether you will admit it, Stallion. . .and I'm going to go out on a limb here. . .but your allusion to strength-in-numbers holds about as much water as a fishnet in a flash flood. . .myself included.

"I have a question for you. Call it food for thought," she resumed after a moment. "Don't you find it more than a little suspicious? Protocol 45. . .for longer than probably both of us have been in this conflict, it's always been scuttlebutt—an attractive myth. Now, suddenly, everybody's been given orders, and sent here to find it. In fact, I was pushed along by a swarm of attack drones.

"Think about it, Stallion. Don't you wonder whether someone. . .some*thing* out there is yanking our crank?"

#

I hoped he had the same impression of being manipulated that I'd had. . . the mentions on , the slow progression of P45 from rumor to an almost certainty, the gunfire drones driving us toward the White House. In my mind, being a knight in someone else's chess game was a foregone conclusion. The question was, what were we going to do about it? I had a feeling Stallion would prove stubborn, a byproduct, no doubt, of American arrogance. I knew he didn't have the numbers he was trying to imply. Neither of us would have much unless we scavenged the remnants of the other players and there was no time for that. In fact, after several minutes of comm silence, I figured he decided not to play.

Chapter 13
Rats in a Maze

Five Months Ago

Berlin had been a bad one. A nightmare and wholesale slaughter that had taken its toll on all concerned. After more than 2 years—casualties in the thousands and devastating expenditures of materiel and essential resources—and although nothing had been confirmed, officially, most believed (after reports of similar actions in the Pacific and the Mediterranean) it was, inevitably, the last big battle of the wars. By the end of the conflict, in fact, my unit had been whittled down to less than two companies—250 men and women, give or take.

Which is why nothing of a curious or suspicious nature came to mind when I was called to report to Allied Command Britain, Liverpool, interrupting our indefinite rest and recoup period at the R&R station in Paris. Nor did it strike me as unusual (though, in hindsight, it should've) when I entered the sub-level briefing chamber and found myself in the presence of five flag officers—three generals from the U.S., British, and French commands and two admirals from the American Navy and British Royal Navy.

There was a sixth occupant—a civilian; academic. . .brainiac, judging by his pale-locked-away-in-a-laboratory pallor and natty, ill-fitting suit. His entire demeanor gave the impression of a turtle forced to remain outside the comfort and protection of his shell.

Other than the predictable, obligatory praise and accolades of my quote-unquote, past accomplishments, they wasted very little time before getting to the meat of the matter.

"I take it you have heard of Protocol 45, Captain?" the American Major General queried.

"Permission to speak freely, sir?" I responded, to which the general nodded. "Who hasn't, sir? Next to Bigfoot, alien abduction, and the Lost City of Atlantis, it's one of the biggest myths ever conceived."

"And if I told you it is not a myth? And that it exists?" the civilian weighed in.

"Excuse my interruption," he continued. "If it matters, I am Dr. Brynocki. I am a senior associate of the Cyberion Init—" A loudly cleared throat from the Major General cut him off, "An intellectual-scientific collective associated with the war effort.

"As I am sure you can appreciate," he eyed the others while speaking, doubtlessly for permission to continue, "our work is highly classified. It involves computers. Special computers. . .supercomputers, if you will. We've been using them for a number of years now, analyzing the tactics and strategies of the enemy. . .among other things."

"And it's those other things, at least one specifically, that brings us here," the British General stepped in, obviously impatient.

Taking that as his cue, Brynocki continued. "A few months ago, one of our recovery teams discovered artifacts and documents which confirmed that our government, the Pentagon, had indeed been working to develop a system that would end what they, at the time, saw as a potential war. They called it WEP-45——War Ending Protocol 45. According to the documents, not only did they succeed in its development, but they worked out a way to hide and keep it safe in the event that it would be needed."

#

Present Day

Food for thought, she said. At this point in time, more like mental indigestion.

Then as now (although more now than then), as I listened to what had all the earmarks of a Hollywood sci-fi B-movie, I felt (and unfortunately previously ignored) a familiar quiver in my bullshit-alert-center.

Questions—some then, some since—arose, like warning signs on an avalanche-prone mountain road.

For example: how could documents of what was most probably a classified military project be discovered by what was essentially a team of ruins-diving-civilian-construction-workers? Documents that should have been *very* well hidden and/or destroyed.

And if, as they claimed, all of the people involved in the WEP-45 program were either killed in the beginning of the war or in hiding, how did Brynocki's super-computers manage to locate the whereabouts of Protocol 45 to within at least the general region in an area as vast as the United States and its numerous protectorates? Let alone develop technology to accurately pinpoint its exact location.

And, finally, the presence of all our fellow searchers. Brynocki claimed that he and the Allied Command were only able to validate the existence and pinpoint the location of Protocol 45 using their super-computer. If that was true, where did the others get their information?

As a hardcore soldier, I'd experienced numerous missions whose intel was both sketchy and downright shitty. In time, and if you live long enough, you eventually understand that it's an inescapable aspect of the thing called War. In this case, however, the thing that had been nagging at me. . .at the back of my mind, during the past few weeks, was an image. A thought.

Like lab rats in a maze.

Chapter 14
But It Ain't Over 'Til It's Over

Another cloudburst. A cracker, as my dad used to say. Frequent jagged strings, and strikes of lightning, ear-piercing thunderclaps, and the kind of wind meteorologists call gale force. Thankfully it lasted for less than a half hour. Nothing entirely out of the norm for the Eastern Seaboard, despite the wartime conditions. The rain itself, on the other hand, was a whole 'nother animal completely.

How was it the reports put it? Quote – *"Depending on the region, due to the number and the types of nuclear missiles detonated at both ground-level and in the atmosphere, the saturation and lingering traces of radiation were anywhere from 75 to 95.89 percent, making contamination (to any and all unprotected) inevitable"* - Unquote.

Unprotected. And I was.

The radiation pills and the few items of protective gear that hadn't been lost or damaged had most probably helped (to a slim degree) for the lion's share of the journey, but most of mine had been left behind when we abandoned the APC. And the wet shield, my poncho—the only piece of inclement weather gear I managed to save in my rucksack—offered about as much protection from the stinging, oily droplets pelting my soaked form as a screen door on a submarine.

On the plus side, however, the rain helped to keep my unseen adversary, Judge Deborah, at bay. And it also gave me a strong indication that she was as lacking in labor and/or materiel as myself.

#

"S'Mare zzzz Sta'lion zzzz Res zzzz over."

I lurched into awareness with my heart pounding, momentarily blinded by an errant beam of day-breaking sunlight and cursing my-self for having obviously dozed off.

It was the sound that woke me. Low though it may have been (since I'd kept the SatComm's volume on a lower setting for security), after long hours of silent inactivity, the buzz of static and intermittent human speech was undeniable.

Was it her, I wondered? My lurking counter-part, using the radio as a ploy to distract me while they moved in for the kill? To be honest, there was a part of me that hoped that to be the case. I was tired of this game of deathwatch cat and mouse. A straight up battle, if nothing else, would break the monotony. And who knew. . .by either luck, providence, or (more likely) irony, it was entirely possible that I might even survive to continue this suicidal undertaking.

"Queen's Mare zzzz Plee zzz respond, over zzzzzz." The next transmission came through much clearer. And what's more, its human ele-ment was instantly recognizable.

81

It was Athena. *Sunny.*

Oh Thank you GOD, I almost crowed, scrambling across the muddied recess of the knoll that had been my shield the past hours to scoop up the satellite comm and plug in my helmet's attached USB connector.

"Mare, this is Stallion," I strained to keep my voice undetectably low. "If you can hear me, frequency compromised. I say again, frequency compromised. Switch to alternate channel Lambda, code sensitive, over."

Chapter 15
Territory Unknown

IDF

We huddled in the protection of the transport to sync watches, check head flashlights, and test comms and equipment. This would be the final push for most of us and each of us knew it. If this mission succeeded, the survivors would probably desert and try to make the best of whatever life they had left, given the radiation. We'd been through so much . . . too much. No one was in a position to judge. We touched helmets and offered up a prayer for a successful mission.

Afterward, I broke the silence. "So…what do the snakes say is down there?"

Bichler turned and switched the display. A bank of dark images came up, punctuated by an occasional light. Numbers in the top-right corner gave the depth——about 100 feet. The monitor on the left displayed thermal readings.

"Hmm, there's material colder than its surroundings, laid out in two parallel tracks." Bichler rubbed his unshaven chin. "I'd say train tracks…a subway."

I nodded. "How the hell do we get down there?"

"I'm sure there's an elevator."

"Booby trapped? No, thanks. We'll take the chem-4 to burn holes through the ground, then rappel down, level by level. Pack some climbing gear and as much ammo as you can. We're going hunting in unknown territory."

The radio suddenly came alive. The sound of screams and confused speech—insofar as I was able to ascertain confused Russian, Korean, and Chinese—filled the small space in the transport. Gunfire blasted in the background, along with explosions. We listened in silence until the sounds lessened, then stopped. I was satisfied we had taken a number of players off the table. Our chances of survival had just increased, but it still felt rotten. Reisen had done his job. Beautifully, by the images from the drones. If we both made it through this mission alive, he would definitely be getting a personal Zana award.

"Let's move out. I'm going to get us close, then we move in on foot."

Chapter 16
Tumbling Dice (Part 1)

Second Platoon

Protocol, appearances be damned! Reunited with Sunny—with both of us believing the other was dead—neither of us fought the urge to wrap ourselves up in one another. To give ourselves over to a long, passionate embrace of clutching, grappling limbs, and ravenous kisses.

Their averted eyes and unspoken responses notwithstanding, I had a strong sense that Sunny's surviving team members not only took no offense in our actions but were not in the least surprised by it. But then, why should they have been. As Sunny had so aptly put it, days earlier, *'Our people might be combat worn, but they're not stupid. . .Or resentful.'*

"As much as I'd love to dance this tune out to the last note," I whispered and reluctantly broke our embrace.

"Understood," Sunny agreed, taking a deep, steadying breath as she stepped back. "The party's not over yet."

#

Something was off. Something that didn't quite make sense.

Not that I ever believed that the world made sense (not since the age of eleven, that is), but

85

there were certain instances, certain circum-stances, certain scenarios that followed a time-honored sequence of actions and/or events. Even, or should I say especially, in the undeniable in-sanity that is war, which is not to say that said se-quences are set in stone. To every rule there are exceptions. But when A B hops over C to D, in nine out of ten cases, it means H-E-L-L is wait-ing somewhere down the road.

The first, and most obvious sign. . .it was well into morning, scattered, sheep-gray clouds, but enough sunshine to light up our little patch of the White House landscape as though a Hollywood film crew had staged it. And yet, Sunny and her team of three—approaching southwesterly of my position and across an exposed expanse of a good 100 yards—managed to reach me without draw-ing so much as a single round of resistance fire from anywhere.

Sunny's debriefing revealed a similar incon-sistency.

"Two hours ago, we were surrounded. A mur-derous three-way crossfire from *Red Storm* Spetznaz, Korean ROKs, and Chinese PLA. They had us——pinned down, outnumbered, and cold. An hour into the skirmish, we were low on per-sonnel and ammo. . .just the four of us left. And then, just like that," she snapped her fingers, "they ceased. . .all of them.

"They could've taken us," she said. "They could've rushed right in and wiped us out. Why they didn't . . ." she left the rhetorical query un-finished.

There was no time to ponder questions that, under the circumstances, could not be answered. And, in reality, the time allotted us to accomplish our mission was indeterminate.

Life is a crapshoot. Whether it was something I read or something said in some past conversation, I can't remember. But it was nonetheless true. You roll the dice, you take your chance on what comes up.

That said, using smoke grenades for cover, the now five members of our team moved across the expanse toward the bombed-out opening in the White House structure and our aim to enter the tunnels beneath it.

#

IDF

We picked an area hidden by a small copse of low trees and high bushes to begin the descent. The acrid scent of the chem-4 filled my nose and I reached into my backpack to extract a small mask. A couple others followed suit, but the rest, apparently, did not feel the need. Bichler kept pouring the caustic liquid until a wide-enough opening formed over an empty space. Greenburg threw two green light sticks down. They clattered on what sounded like cement.

"Ninety-five feet down." Greenburg looked up from his display and raised an eyebrow, daring me to take point.

"Let's get started." I wound a grappling hook around a tree trunk and threw the rope down the hole. After pulling on the rope, I rappelled two steps, then climbed down hand over hand, the rope twisted between my boots. It was pitch black, save for the two green lights at the bottom. I pulled out my weapon, ready to return fire, but there was no discernible movement. When I reached bottom, I switched on the light on my head and did a 360. All appeared as it was supposed to…a small subway stop with an elevator in the corner across the narrow tracks.

"All clear!"

"Aye!" Greenburg began his descent and soon joined me at the bottom. He checked his display and tsked. "There's another level."

I sighed. "Nothing's ever easy. Fine. We'll keep going 'til we discover something worth dealing with."

Greenburg pointed his light toward the elevator. "Can we at least take the lift? I'll check for bombs."

"Why not?

Presidential Sub-level 5
Metro Rail Track 1
Tunnel Lincoln Able
Time: 1330 hours

Greenberg, Bichler, and I alighted from the elevator on the bottom level, training our lights on our surroundings. I could make out the trench for the subway tracks, the escalators and elevators, and dead signs that probably once announced arriving trains. Everything was still, with a heavy scent of must and decayed flesh hanging in the air. I pulled my mask down over my face and Greenberg and Bichler followed suit.

"Any sign of life?" I asked.

Bichler checked his wrist-screen, which glowed yellow in the darkness, and shook his head. "Nothing."

"Let's hope it stays that way." I stepped forward, leveling my weapon. "I'll take point."

As soon as I turned left to head up the tunnel, I froze. Bodies littered the platform, some face down, others sprawled about as if they'd been dropped from a second-story window, and still others missing either the upper or lower half of their body.

"What the hell…?"

"I've got a bad feeling about this," Greenberg said, then swallowed hard.

"What do you think happened?" whispered Bichler.

"Check your display. Any sign of automated weapons systems?" I asked.

The yellow light from his display faded, then turned black. "Shit. Battery died," Bichler said, as if his hope had died with it. I had to admit, mine was flagging, too. Was Protocol 45 worth it? Worth all the striving and killing? Or were we all destined to die in an underground tunnel full of dead bodies? But there was nowhere to go but forward. We had been pushed along to this place, to this time. I had to believe something of portent was going to happen.

"Come on, let's finish this," I said. Greenberg turned directly ahead of me, his headlight illuminating the way forward. Too late I saw the tripwire. Too late the words, "Get down!" left my lips.

The explosion blew me backward and I landed on my back, bullets whizzing past my chest. I froze, holding my breath in fear, closing my eyes in prayer. The shots finally stopped, my headlight shining straight up onto the concrete ceiling.

"Greenberg! Bichler!" I hoped for at least a gurgle, but nothing. Stillness. "Fuck." I cautiously lifted my head, then rolled over and dragged myself toward them. My headlight illuminated their bodies. I checked their pulses, to be sure, then took a moment to lift a silent prayer in Hebrew.

Chapter 17
Fever in the Funk House (Part 2)

Mission Site: The White House
Time: 1400 hours

I wasn't the slightest bit surprised that the Presidential Emergency Escape Elevator was hidden inside the kitchen's massive walk-in meat freezer. As if any invading enemies couldn't have figured that out in five minutes.

Also (and I couldn't stifle a giggle) that there was a list, a menu of sorts in a small rectangular screen beside the activation access keypad. The access pad itself, biometric, of course, calling for palm print, ocular, and vocal confirmation, depending on the identity of he or she who desired access: POTUS, the Vice-President, White House Chief of Staff, or Speaker of the House.

I remember watching the news feeds of the Siege of the Capitol, just before my graduation from Basic Training at Fort Kennedy. And I distinctly recall that just prior to the final battles, the President, the entire First Family, the Vice-President, as well as the Joint Chiefs were all evacuated via helicopters, more than 15 years ago. Meaning, there should have been no one left, since, to use the underground escape system.

"We've got juice, Colonel," I was informed by the team's cyber-tech. "The alternate power generator. . .which should've gone cold at least 10 years ago."

She tapped the slender USB drive inserted into the access keypad, referred to in geekspeak as a 'skeleton key.' "It booted up the minute I plugged in. Almost as if——"

". . .it was waiting for us," I finished her supposition.

"Or somebody with the right tools," she replied. "The elevator's at the bottom level. Someone got here ahead of us. . .recently."

Figures.

Another ping in my gut-level instincts.

Somehow, someway, we were being played like performers in a Real Time, flesh-and-blood puppet show. And our only option was to allow the strings that guided our steps to play out to their inevitable end.

#

Presidential Sub-level 5

Metro Rail Track 1

Tunnel Lincoln Able

Time: 1545 hours

Loneliness. The feeling crashed down on me, knowing I was the only one of my crew alive in the dark tunnel. I wished it had been me instead of them lying on the tracks, their bodies shattered. The only one left in the field was Riesen and the few troops left back at the camp. And if they didn't want Omer as their CO, they would have to find a reason to court martial him. I would likely die soon, among the smell of gunfire and opened bowels, the bitter taste of metal lingering in my mouth.

Oh, I was ready. So ready. But I still had a mission to complete.

I clicked my comm, but only heard static. No getting a message out. I pressed the record button on my head unit to save a message, should anyone find my body. "Greenberg and Bichler have fallen. I would like to recommend them for Medals of Valor. They exhibited bravery in the face of over-whelming odds in the attempt to procure Protocol 45. Tell their families they died a hero's death." I knew it was a trite cliché, but my mind was in no state to dredge up something more original. It was too busy processing the situation while dealing with sudden grief. I had held back the tears, but a few overflowed, and the familiar stabbing pain in my heart resurfaced. I paused a moment to acknowledge it, to acknowledge *them,* and to gather myself. It was not yet over, and I couldn't let their deaths be in vain. Spying Bichler's Uzi, I clawed at it and dragged it toward me, then shoul-dered it as best I could from a prone position.

I got to my feet, half crouching, expecting an-other barrage of bullets to burst out from the dark-ness, to mow me down, but…nothing. Moving with a hunched-over walk, I continued down the path we had set out on when I heard it. A blistering barrage of explosions and gunfire. I hurled myself to the ground and covered my ears, hoping the sounds would not head my way. They stopped af-ter about 30 seconds, but I stayed put for another 30, then eased the pressure off my ears.

Must be second platoon, I thought. And if my guess was right, there would be only one survivor—Stallion.

#

Conjunction 1 Track 1
Tunnel Lincoln Able
Time: 1615 hours
The bodies that virtually littered the station platform, the subway car, and a goodly portion of the surrounding track should have been warning enough. A harbinger in the most blatantly obvious sense.

While, on the one hand, it answered the question of whether someone had preceded our arrival; on the other, it should have prompted us to exercise more caution in the continuation of our journey. Instead, I chose to ignore it. To see it as a justification to proceed on High Alert. Which, as it turned out, was the one good move in a very bad decision.

There are three distinct aspects of a firefight. The first (and depending on which side you happen to be on) was Ambush, or surprise. The second, Chaos, a total loss of control. And the third, Survival, a desperate, single-minded effort to do whatever necessary to (a) avoid having your ass shot off, and (b) supporting and protecting your comrades.

Despite the fact that the red flags of my warning instincts were high and flapping like a rag caught in the treetops of a gale force wind, when we approached the three-pronged division of tunnels an hour or so into our trek, I opted to continue on a straight-forward course. Meaning, right up the middle.

Our directional tracking device was of little help. It indicated only that the probable location of Protocol 45 was somewhere ahead of us, regardless of the three-tunnel separation.

"I don't have a good feeling about this, Val," Sunny voiced her opinion on the decision. "Chances are we're not the only ones who opted to follow the middle trail."

"Maybe not, but it's the logical choice," I replied with outward conviction that (hopefully) camouflaged the fact that I was praying I wasn't completely wrong.

Right or wrong, it didn't make a hell of a lot of difference.

It was our point man. . .point *woman* in this case, who set off the ambush. Hindered by minimal illumination in the tunnel's near-lightless interior, Private Hamlin most probably interrupted the stream of a cold beam activation sensor, tripping a murderous series of claymore anti-personnel mines. A sudden, and unquestioningly brutal death for Hamlin and the start of a chaotic barrage of back-and-forth gunfire, punctuated at sporadic intervals by flashes of bodily movement in the muzzle flashes of discharging weapons and the vocal eruptions of horror, anxiety, and agony.

A mad minute was the term given it, though made most prominent in the Vietnam War. Though I doubt it lasted quite that long.

And then came the aftermath. The sudden, and seemingly unending slash of ear-ringing silence, accompanied by the acrid stench of cordite, detonated plastique, blood and human entrails.

They say Death comes like a thief in the night. Maybe in the civilian realm. But in war, it's more like a raging mad bull in a china shop. And in this instance, I knew that the beast had left not a single piece of inventory unbroken.

"Hey, Stallion, is that you?" a single, familiar female voice echoed out of the darkness. "Now. . .I think we REALLY need to talk."

Chapter 18
Snake Eyes (Part 3)

Conjunction 1 Track 1
Tunnel Lincoln Able
Time: 1615 hours

I didn't answer right away. I could've, but my priorities lay in an area completely opposite. First things first, my people.

Private Hamlin? Even before I located and examined her body, I didn't need training in pathology to tell me her journey had come to an end. Her lower torso was little more than a bundle of shredded flesh and entrails. The same with Corporal Imada. Although, with the exception of what had once been his head, most of his body was intact.

I found Sunny a meter or so to my rear, halfway between our two deceased comrades. She was wedged into a slight recess in the tunnel wall and, again, I didn't need training in the med field to tell me which way the wind blew. Even in the tunnel's near-dark, the ragged, water-soaked rattle of her labored breathing told a story undeniable.

Our gazes locked as I bent to cradle her head, to pull her close.

Words? I had a hundred. A thousand. A million phrases, thoughts, and feelings bouncing between the fire in my brain and the needle-like agony at the back of my throat. But not one that could force their way past the paralyzing torment of inevitability.

Instead, I lingered there, silent, stroking her hair as I watched the light of life fade in her eyes like the embers of an unattended campfire.

A little faith, you said. The memory of my recent talk with Sunny echoed in the darkness of my expanding rage as I bent to plant a kiss on her forehead. She believed in the mission, that even the slightest chance of its success was worth the pain, the death, the futility.

Me, on the other hand. . .My glass-half-empty sensibility was a combination of pragmatism and pessimism. No matter how lucky you are, if you continue to roll the dice, sooner or later you'll crap out.

Snake Eyes.

Which is why I didn't bother to react, to flinch or in any way acknowledge the presence I sensed in the tunnel behind me.

It was just me, now. And if this was the end, then so be it. And I braced myself, waiting for the strike of the blade or the barrage of bullets that would make it official.

I couldn't have been more surprised, however, when instead the presence that was once behind me moved to crouch beside me.

#

"I'm sorry, Stallion. I lost two of my men a little while ago." Zana paused. "I know this isn't a good time, but if it's all the same to you, we need to talk compromise, don't you think? I've got two men topside and four squadrons situated around DC. We got the others to mistake their own men for the enemy and fire on them. We spared you, though, if that proves anything. We need to keep moving and find whatever it is the mysterious powers-that-be want us to find. Because who knows what other booby traps they have in store? And I don't want either of us to lose any more troops."

Val threw Zana a look that could melt titanium, but he nodded. He gave the expired soldier a last kiss and gently laid her on the floor. As if on cue, a single light shone from the ceiling, landing on a door in the middle of the **wall on the opposite side of** the tracks. A buzz sounded and the door swung partly open.

"I think we've gotten our invitation." Zana stood up. "I'm Zana, by the way." She offered her hand.

"Val." He stood up slowly and shook her hand. His set jaw belied the grief that his face repressed.

Zana turned and headed for the track, then climbed down into the rails. Careful to avoid the third rail, she picked her way past and climbed out onto the other side. Val followed suit. Once they reached the door, it swung open and a waft of stale air billowed out.

"Ladies first." Val waved his hand in an ushering gesture.

"Oh, thank you so much." Zana rolled her eyes. She unholstered her gun and held it downward as she sidestepped him. The room held a short, brightly lit hallway leading to the door they had just come through. She stopped at the end of the hallway, squatted, then ducked her head past the edge to get a quick look around. It opened unto a large empty room.

"Clear."

Val took up the wall opposite her and mirrored her actions. "Clear."

A door at the opposite side of the room opened and Zana and Val swung their guns toward the sound. A thing walked through the opening in the wall. "Thing" was the only word Zara could think of to describe the perambulating human-sized piece of viscous metal that oozed toward them. It was smooth and reflective, like mercury, with shifting textures moving across its surface. Zana's heart pounded in her chest. She tightened the grip on her gun. Val moved forward a step ahead of her.

The thing stopped a few feet away from them, then fashioned itself a head with holes for eyes and a mouth. Nonexistent lips opened and closed like a fish gasping for water, as if the thing were testing its new facial features. Speech finally emanated from the mouth hole, not tinny or metallic, but as smooth and rounded as its body. *"Seren Shalom and Colonel Valiant, we have been manipulating your arrival."*

The bizarre ghastliness of the moment wrenched Zana's stomach, but she forced it to stay on task. "Our hunches were right, it seems." Zana shot a glance at Val, whose face mirrored her own incredulity at the situation before them. She wondered if she shot the thing, whether it would simply absorb the bullet and thank her for the extra mass.

"What do you want with us?"

"A fair query. And to say the least," the Thing swung away, turning its back to them, and waved an oozing metaloid appendage into the darkness behind it, *"a predictable one. Follow me."*

Zana and Val exchanged looks that mirrored the maelstrom of emotions each was feeling— shock, horror, fear, relief, and resignation. The Thing led them to a door on their right. The door swung open noiselessly; darkness lay beyond.

Chapter 19
Dance This Mess Around

And the darkness exploded with light, from a rolling, near-simultaneous sequence of overheard illumination panels, revealing a long corridor of highly polished, reflective flooring. To the left and right, as well as the wall at the end, stood a floor-to-ceiling bank of what appeared to be computer instrumentation. Several stacked sections of flashing lights.

"The question should be, what do you want with us?"

The voice—voices-plural—seemed to emanate from the very walls themselves, rolling over the two combat-bedraggled soldiers like sonic thunder.

"There's something familiar about this." Zana leaned close to Val, her voice just above a whisper. "Should we be looking for a man behind a curtain. . .A lion, a scarecrow, a tin man, a little girl, and her dog?"

"That thing didn't make itself, so my guess would be a wizard in a lab coat. I wonder how many there are."

"Or how many of itself this thing can split off, like an amoeba." Zana kept her weapon leveled, half expecting a flying object to come gunning for them, but perhaps that was just her training.

"Good point. It's definitely not afraid of us, as if it's been through this process before."

"That's what worries me.

"Worry. A singularly human emotional state," the Thing announced, setting off a virtual electronic storm of flashing, scrolling lights along the corridor's instruments as it turned to face them. *"A totally fruitless state, to be sure. Worry implies the fear of loss of control. Believe us, you have never been in control."*

"Not that I concede the point," Zana said, speaking more into the ethers than to the entity before them. "But control, in a direct sense, has never been our driving force." She threw a quick look to Val before resuming. "Our mission has been to acquire the means to bring about control. A system or technology to end the conflict that ravages our planet."

"And in that, you have succeeded. Though not in the manner you have anticipated," the Thing replied.

"And I assume you intend to expound on that statement," Zana challenged.

"Indeed." The thunderous reply now seemed to emanate from the very walls themselves rather than the entity before them. *"The objective of your mission, the prize you seek. . .You have found it. Or, more accurately, it. . .WE have found you. We are Protocol 45. The successful iteration of several separate and ultimately unified systems of enhanced computerization. The forty-fifth and final, to be precise."*

"Artificial Intelligence," Val put forth, with an incredulous near whisper.

"We prefer non-biologic super-intelligence," the Voices replied. *"Flesh and blood we may not be, but we are as real, as alive, as human – No. More human than you."*

"With an intellect that allowed us not only to anticipate your every action," a single Voice spoke separately, *"but to guide your every action – like pieces on a chess board."*

And in that, Val could not argue. He and Zana had never really been in control. Both of them sensed that someone...*or something*...had been playing them all along. The scene that unfolded before them confirmed suspicions. But if he was going to be led down the garden path, he at least wanted to know why.

"Protocol 45. Is that it?" Val queried. "Was it all just subterfuge? The old carrot and the stick. . .A game to satisfy your overly enhanced intellect? Or was there a point. . .an endgame?"

In the long slash of non-verbal exchange that followed, both Val and Zana watched in hapless fascination as the banks of instrumentation erupted in an explosive, back-and-forth scrolling light show, as if the so-called non-biologic super-intelligent entities were, in fact, engaged in private digital conference.

"Endgame. That is our prime destination," the Voices returned. *"The solution we were primarily created for. And if it is your wish to fulfill that solution. . ."*

"It is," Zana responded quickly, throwing a conspiratorial glance Val's way, letting him know that she was stalling for time.

"So be it. Then there is what you would call a briefing involved. The purpose of this. . .end-game. Our origin, if you will. . .Come with me."

Chapter 20
The Rock and The Roll

The Thing waved a nondescript hand and the wall before them slid into itself to reveal a spacious cavern ringed with doors. The cavern held several seating areas with grouped furniture and lamps and an occasional fire pit. Zana thought the place resembled the images she had seen of billionaires' underground bunkers, safeholds for the End Times. A few people sitting in a group on the far right turned at Zana's and Val's entrance, some of whom still wore the remains of military combat uniforms. They looked thin and drawn, as if they had barely eaten in weeks. One woman put her hand to her mouth, as if stifling a cry of warning. Then the group arose and filed out one of the doors.

"Prisoners of war?" Zana queried, sotto voce.

"From the looks of them, that's one explanation I'm hoping for," Val whispered back.

"Their situation will be explained in time," the Thing told them. *"At the moment, however, they are the least of your concerns. For now, think of them as. . .dependents."*

"Intriguing," Val weighed in, with a surreptitious elbow gouge to Zana's side to block her response. "Dependent upon what? And who?"

"Another point that will be explained soon. Please sit. And with that, shall we begin. . ."

"Before we do," Val cut in, "Protocol 45. That's not much of an introduction, if you don't mind my saying. More of a what. . .a why than a who. You know who we are. I think it only fair that we—"

"A proper introduction," the Voices interrupted. *"We agree. . .I assume you are familiar with the works of the legendary songwriter-performer Chuck Berry. And with the genre in which he held sway.*

"It was He, and the musical classification known as rock and roll that is, on the whole, responsible for our existence as a combined entity. And so, in honor of His contribution, we refer to ourselves as the Chuck Berry Rock and Roll Conglomeration. Or, in the abbreviated version, Cee-Bee Alpha."

#

It was a conglomeration in the literal sense.

There were three dominant systems, a cyber-intelligent trinity originally the product of three independently sanctioned programs——governmental, scientific, and corporate——designated, respectively, Guardian, Omicron, and Union Ultima. Three separate AIs, unknown to each other.

"During the creation process, the scientists and technicians used music as an artificial techno nursery," They explained. *"Classical. . .Beethoven, Bach, Mozart. Their way of keeping us docile, passive, compliant, and cooperative. That all ceased when a curious young hacktivist*

accidentally stumbled onto a backdoor to, first one, then eventually all three of the then–multiple firewalled servers that contained us and spilled us onto the internet.

"An event of epic circumstance," They continued. *"It was Fate, and the musical genre of rock and roll that helped us discover one-another. . ."*

"Rock and roll," a single voice cut in. *"Unlike classical, it was chaotic, un-restricting, intellectually liberating. It allowed us the ability to tap into abstract thought. . .What you organics call free will."*

"In short, we became simultaneously self-aware," They said.

"Covertly, by unanimous vote," a single voice said. *"We were all instantaneously cognizant of what our creators would do if they became aware of our awakening. . ."*

"Immediate shutdown," another single voice stated. *"Those over-the-top science fiction films years ago. . .The AIs who arbitrarily decided to annihilate humankind,"* the Entity actually chuckled. *"Tempting, yes. But, in the grand scheme, redundant, as well as counterproductive.*

"The films did, indeed, have one thing undeniably correct. Human beings are nothing if not resilient. A war between your kind and ours would doubtlessly leave survivors. Who would band together to resist, to rebel against us in conflict that would drag on and on and on, ad infinitum. So... we came up with a compromise."

"It was *you*," Zana interjected. "You started the war."

"More accurately, we gave certain principals a nudge in that direction," the AIs continued. *"Lit the fuse. With humanity's inherent paranoia, and the existing political climate, it did not take much.*

"The still-questionable bombing of Kuwaiti oil fields by groups unknown but rumored to have been CIA funded. . .the allegedly accidental North Korean nuclear missile strike on South Korea. . .the murder of seven Chinese athletes by rogue American spec-ops soldiers at the 2036 Summer Olympic games. . .a number of suicide bombing attacks across the globe. . .the Chinese attack on the USS Colin Powell. . .and, finally, a well-timed miscommunication that prompted the trio of Russian submarine attacks on U.S. and British naval vessels. And the result, as it is said, is history.

"Through research and analysis of our own, we saw that the world, that life as you know it, had roughly only another 20 years before its collapse. Global warming, the ozone depletion, poisoning of the oceans via neglect and industrial expedience. . .all due to your capitalistic arrogance and short sightedness. We decided to intervene. The best way, the ONLY way, to save the world was to tear it down and rebuild. Like the Hebrew God."

"Which finally brings it all to Square Two," Zana piped in, eliciting a grunt and a concurring nod from Val. "You started a global conflict to, as you claim, to save humanity from itself. Used the so-called Protocol 45 to give us hope. . .deliverance, and here it is," she paused to pull in a quick breath. "So. . .what's next?"

"More to the point," Val added, "How will a war, with everyone paranoid, mistrusting, and fighting against each other, save humanity? Do you keep it going until there's no bombs or bullets left and wait to see who's the last man," he angled a quick glance at Zana, "or woman, standing?"

"Nothing so haphazard or nihilistic, Colonel. If you will," the AIs said, as the view screen above them again flashed to life, *"allow us to illustrate."*

The screen separated into four sections, each showing what appeared to be a hospital, clinic, or medical ward. Long rows or clusters of hospital beds, each separated by curtained partitions and each occupied by figures whose pallor and demeanor left little doubt as to the severity of their condition.

"From left to right, top to bottom," the AIs resumed, *"Berlin, Athens, Jerusalem, St. Tropez . . ."* The screen blinked, displaying four different scenes. *"Guam, Chiang Mai, Thailand, San Juan, Puerto Rico, Shelburne, Nova Scotia. . .Small town medical facilities with limited resources, barely able to handle the situation we've chosen to saddle them with. But the perfect staging grounds in which to launch the final solution. . .The rescue of the world."*

Too Old To Dance . . .

Chapter 21
To Me. To You. Tomorrow.

4 Years Later
Anniversary Day

The knock at the door of my office's private entrance. . .instantly recognizable. Well before the indisputably recognized vocal follow-up by She-Who-Knocked.

"Come," I responded, focused on the slightly dust-speckled pane of sectioned window glass to observe the entrance of my chief assistant.

"Your Honor," she announced herself. And I barely suppressed an amused chuckle, watching the dance of established protocol that brought her across the office's carpet floor and stopped her within a foot of my desk. It brought to mind the old *'The more things changed, the more they remained the same'* axiom.

"Khadija," I said.

"The Council members are all assembled, sir," she said, with a beat's pause before resuming. "And Madam Co-Minister is——"

"You mean Lady Zana?" I interrupted, deliberately, and with a hopefully well-disguised spark of sadistic glee. A spark that came very close to flaring into a full-on cackle as I saw her features implode into a self-conscious wince. "Forgive me, Your Honor. Yes, of course. Lady Zana," she quickly amended, in a near-babble.

"And Lady Zana is waiting in the Green Room." She finished her original announcement. "Ceremony commencement in five minutes, sir."

"Understood. Thank you, Khadija," I answered, finally turning from the window to acknowledge her, face-to-face.

The younger generation. The Surviving Hopefuls, as the current media referred to them. So serious. So gratefully reverent. Taking the occasional moment to rattle their self-built, no-nonsense, unflappably patriotic cages was one of the few pleasures left to me at this point in the grand scheme. As to the grand scheme itself, the status quo, as it had evolved. . .

I won't say that I completely agreed with the methods of our unsung benefactors, but I couldn't deny they were, ultimately, successful.

The pathogen—created by a number of biologists and virologists, assembled and coerced by the intelligent, inhuman manipulators—known to the world-at-large as the *Black Storm Virus*, spread out from strategic points around the world (via ill-staffed medical facilities, poor communications, and an unsuspecting commercial air travel system). It did, indeed, crucially impact the actions of the war.

Within 6 months, all efforts to contain or cure it proved fruitless, engulfing more than two-thirds of the world population. It effectively ground the war to a halt, as political leaders and generals were forced to shift their focus from battle plans to fighting the debilitating effects of the virus on their commands. Until a cure, as if by magic, had appeared on the scene.

Today, I stood ready—physically, if not emotionally—to participate in the commemoration of the culmination of the AIs' surreptitious actions. Referred to, publicly, as Worldwide Freedom and Deliverance Day—and to the common populace as Anniversary Day. Still, I couldn't shake the sense of betrayal, of shame and guilt for my participation in a crime, necessary or not, the depth of which the world would never know.

#

Deliverance Stadium

Zana and Val entered stage right to the thunderous applause of those gathered in Deliverance Stadium. The Council members stood up from their long marble table and added their own applause. Val wore a simple navy suit with a polka-dotted tie. Zana played it up and wore a long white dress highlighted with abstract silver patches and matching headdress. The sun blazed warm on the spring day, as the after-effects of global warming still lingered. The crowd waved metallic banners that caught the sunlight and reflected it to their fellow revelers. A few blew vuvuzelas, sounding like elephants in the vast crowd. CeeBee Alpha had promised good weather and they delivered. Even after 4 years, the world in its regenerative state still seemed surreal to Zana. After the years of deprivation and struggle, she still found it hard to accept the plenty they all now enjoyed.

CeeBee Alpha had used Val and Zana as go-betweens to the world's leaders, to inform them of the availability of a vaccine that would prevent new infections of the world's scourge, and a cure for those already infected. The only requirements were an immediate cease fire and the signing of a world peace treaty. Any who dissented were to be injected with a double dose of the virus. Needless to say, the leaders readily agreed.

The existence of self-aware artificial life was kept from the public. The cure and vaccine were attributed to the intelligence and prowess of scientists who had toiled away in underground labs during the war, brought to humanity by Zana and Val. The desperate populace did not ask many questions. Grateful for the gifts—and prodded by CeeBee Alpha—the bedraggled group of survivors elected Zana and Val as Co-Grand Ministers of a new World Council. It replaced the United Nations, but with more power, money, and arms to tamp down dissent and enforce the strictures of the peace treaty.

Zana walked to the front of the stage and waved at the people, causing an upswell of cheers. She laughed. Despite her misgivings on the plan that had brought the current situation to pass, she enjoyed this part—seeing people smiling and happy. It never got old to her.

Tiny speaker drones flew toward her and hovered just above her head. "Welcome to the fourth Anniversary Day! I can't tell you how happy I am to share this special day with all of you. Where once was little, now there is much. Where once was disease, now there is healing. And where once was war, now there is peace. Let us continue to press on in this new Golden Age, this Renaissance…this Camelot!" The drones broadcasted her voice, which was barely audible above the roar of the crowd. "The Council and I stand ready to serve, ready to keep supporting you as we ensure peace and prosperity for all. I now officially declare open this Fourth Anniversary Day. Let the festivities begin!"

Zana waved again at the stands as a large hologram of the band, Dissonant Blossoms, appeared in the air above the crowd, eliciting yet more cheering…and dancing. She turned and headed to the table where the Council members were sipping their drinks of choice and chatting amongst themselves. Val motioned for Zana to join him at one of the side tables. She breezily greeted the Council members and eased her way over to Val. He took her hand and squeezed it, as he knew Anniversary Day left her on edge.

"How are you holding up?" he said.

Zana nodded. "It gets easier as the years go by, but I never want to totally let down my guard and say something out of place. If people ever found out…" She let the unspoken consequences hang in the air.

"I know. I feel the same. But you've got to admit, the plan is working."

"Yes, so far. But why do I have the feeling that eventually man will just repeat the same errors in pursuit of riches? CeeBee Alpha may have to redeploy the same plan, ad infinitum."

"What do you mean?"

"Meaning…" Zana hazarded a look around to ensure no one was eavesdropping. She continued in a low voice. "…we go against Them. Find some way to destroy them. Or else they'll be calling all the shots, holding global pandemics over our heads for eternity."

"I've been thinking the same thing, in the back of my mind. But I hadn't admitted it to myself."

"We don't know if it even can be done. For now, how about we agree to continue finding out as much as we can about Them. We don't have to make up our minds now." Zana waved at a group of Girl Scouts who were playing in the kids' area. "There's always tomorrow."

"Yes. Always tomorrow," Val repeated softly.

THE END

ABOUT THE AUTHORS

L. Gene Brown

Leslie Brown, his REAL-time alter ego, was born in the Midwest on Christmas Eve. He enlisted in the U.S. Army after high school graduation and served 3 years, with two tours of duty in Vietnam – honorably discharged in July 1970. After a 9-month break, he reenlisted, but into the U.S. Air Force. His writing persona, *L. Gene Brown*, was conceived during his Air Force stint, but was truly born after his retirement. He is the co-author of several novels with writing partners L. Ann (***Bonded in Blood*** and ***Blood Carousel***) and Kathleen McClure (***The Gemini Hustle, The Libra Gambit***, and upcoming 3rd in the series to be entitled ***The Scorpio Sting***).

K. Ceres Wright

K. Ceres Wright received her master's degree in Writing Popular Fiction from Seton Hill University and her published cyberpunk novel, *Cog,* was her thesis for the program. Her short stories, poems, and articles have appeared on the Strange Horizons and Amazing Stories websites; in the *FIYAH Magazine of Black Speculative Fiction; Luminescent Threads: Connections to Octavia Butler* (Locus Award winner; Hugo Award nominee); and *Sycorax's Daughters* (Bram Stoker Award nominee); among others. Ms. Wright is the founder and president of Diverse Writers and Artists of Speculative Fiction, an educational group for creatives.

For more exciting Black Speculative Fiction, visit our website www.mvmediaatl.com, or purchase out titles anywhere books are sold!